The Souls Guide to the After Death

a novella

By

GWENNA LAITHLAND

ISBN: 979-8-9925759-0-3 (Paperback)
ISBN: 979-8-9925759-1-0 (Ebook)

Book Cover by Mila Book Covers
Formatting by Amit Dey

First edition 2025.

The After Death is the space that exists between life and death. As such you may encounter any of the following while your guide assists you through the process. Sensitive readers please take note of death, dying, grief, loss, domestic violence, emotional abuse, sexual abuse, sexual harassment, child abuse, child injury, violence against women, violence against children, weaponization of sex, sexuality, panic attacks shown on page, and some light religious deconstructive themes discussed.

DEDICATION

To anyone who has ever felt unfixable.
To everyone willing to be someone's villain.

There was the spot on the tablecloth.

It was an almost-imperceptible, irregular blob of maroon, perhaps a drip of wine or splotch of sauce. It shouldn't have mattered. But Susan Chambers had perceived the almost imperceptible and it soured her mood immediately.

This was the meeting of her career.

It could alter the trajectory of her already upwardly mobile life. This meeting could take her slow-but-steady rise to the top and slap booster rockets on it.

A fat contract for a Department of Defense recruitment ad campaign was there for the taking.

Convincing kids to sign away a few years of their life in defense of their country? The copy basically wrote itself. All she had to do was get a stuffy old man with the personality of damp cardboard to agree that Susan Chambers and her team at Abernathy Ad Executives were the correct choice to convince the next generation to enlist.

And there was a spot on the damn tablecloth.

Susan waved over someone who looked unimportant enough to be waitstaff. A guy with neck tattoos poking out of his stark black button-up came trotting over with the enthusiasm of a golden retriever.

"What can I help you with, ma'am?" Susan spent a long time drinking in the boy. Muscled in all the places she liked them muscled, svelte in all the places she liked them svelte. She let her visual inspection stretch to an inappropriate length of time. It was clear the waiter was getting uncomfortable under the weight of her stare. Good.

His name tag read Tad. Of course his name was Tad.

"Tad?"

"Yes, ma'am."

"Is Grammercy Tavern no longer concerned with a quality guest experience?" Susan cooed, swapping the intense staring with the sensual, husky voice that worked on pretty much every male aged sixteen to seventy-five.

Tad stuttered but managed. "N-No ma'am. Our customer service and guest experience are just as important as the culinary wonder provided by our world-class chefs." Susan was impressed he'd pulled that out of himself. It meant absolutely nothing, but it sounded profound.

Susan slid down the chair just a bit, elongating herself to highlight the curve of her waist and press her chest up toward Tad. They weren't as perky as they used to be, but she'd found most men didn't rightly care once they were allowed to play with them. Susan might have celebrated her forty-second birthday a few months back, but plenty of folks preferred their goods carefully aged. She stared up at Tad through her lashes.

"Oh. That's…" Susan trailed off, letting a finger glide around the lip of her water goblet, "…unfortunate." She watched his eyes dip to her body and flick right back up. His Adam's apple bobbed once. Twice. God, she had him absolutely writhing, and it was glorious. "In my industry, we have a little saying: 'show, don't tell.' And I hear you telling me that my experience is important. But you showed me something different."

Tad scanned the table and then Susan. His face scrunched just a little and the bird wing tattooed on his throat fluttered as his pulse rose. He didn't see it. He didn't see what had Susan on the attack. Delicious. Susan fiddled with the powder-blue edge of her Veronica Beard blazer, sneaking a glance at her watch. As fun as the game was, she didn't have time to see just how long she could string the boy along.

"Are you in the habit of seating guests at tables that have not been properly cleaned?" Susan let her hand float down, a perfectly manicured French Tip landing at the edge of the almost-imperceptible spot. Tad let loose the breath he must have been holding as his shoulders fell.

Susan was enraptured by the cascade of emotions that washed over his face. Frustration, relief, and annoyance each had their moment upon his features. But where was the anger? Where was the evidence that Tad had, for just a moment, considered telling her off or flipping the table or ripping off his stupid, skinny matte-black tie and storming out of this pretentious restaurant, a string of curses trailing behind him? That was the part that enthralled Susan about marketing: the manipulation. Her innate ability to make people feel what she told them to feel.

She'd been in marketing for more than twenty years, and she still felt a unique delight in commanding someone else's emotions. She hadn't gotten Tad all the way to anger like she'd hoped, but she was out of time, and she did need this tablecloth disaster resolved. Phil, the man with all that Department of Defense ad money to toss around, would be arriving in fifteen minutes or so. Straightening in her chair, she sharpened her voice again.

"Tad, are you going to stand there or are you going to show me that Grammercy Tavern has a single shit left to give about their patrons?" There it was. A flash ignited behind Tad's eyes, like a little nuclear detonation in his skull. Anger. God, she was fucking good.

"Of course. We'll resolve this immediately." Tad smoothed his face into a contrite mask. "Would you prefer a different table, or would you like us to change the tablecloth for one that meets your exacting standards?" Susan detected the barb but decided to let him have it.

"I think, for time's sake, I'll take a different table. That one?" Susan pointed to a table tucked away along one of the walls. Far more intimate and less prone to interruption by the other patrons. It was an ideal table for a lunch meeting, and Susan wanted it. What Susan wanted, Susan normally got.

"All yours, then. Please, may I carry your bag?"

"No. I prefer my tablecloths and my bags unmarred, thank you." The anger and irritation sparkled in Tad's swampwater brown eyes like little fireworks. The waiter wordlessly escorted her to the table she'd selected and made his way back up to the front podium to tell the host of the change in seating.

Phil arrived just as Susan had gotten herself resettled.

"Susan Chambers! How the fuck are you, you greedy little bitch?" Susan's mouth fell open in mock affront.

"Doing well, you wrinkled, old, impotent clown!" He met this with a guffaw that might have been embarrassing if Susan hadn't been expecting it. Phil was one of the last bastions of old-school marketing men, a proponent of the good ol' boy system, with all its locker-room talk and overly aggressive handshakes. Being a woman made it slightly more difficult to convince him of anything, but it also made him that much more predictable. And Susan would've been lying if she said she didn't enjoy the challenge.

All she had to do was stroke his pitiful little ego and parrot his own behavior back at him. If he broke out the name calling, she met him blow for blow. He viewed it as some sort of flattery and melted in her hands. It was pathetic, but she was able to use it to her advantage, at least. Susan and Phil had been going back and forth for weeks on the specs of the marketing proposal. He picked through every letter, period, comma, and line break of the pitch, demanding explanation or example.

It was exhausting, but for the ten-digit budget the Department of Defense had allotted for advertising, she answered every damn question. And then answered them again in a new way. It had all led up to this meeting at Grammercy Tavern at the hand-selected table with the perfectly white tablecloth.

"Let's get down to brass tacks, Phil." Susan had no idea what the phrase meant, but he seemed to like when she said shit like that. Brass tacks it was, then.

It took less than an hour—forty-seven minutes, to be precise. Susan was taking a sip of her grapefruit spritzer over the remnants of the most delicious Caesar salad when Phil leaned back in his chair, his knees drifting apart. Susan fought to not let her lips betray her disgust. Smacking his palms on his thighs, he puffed air through his lips with a slight hiss.

"Alright, Susan. I'm going to level with you. What you're offering here, what you say you can do, boy, I'll tell you." Phil really liked hearing himself talk. Leaning forward, he slammed his elbows onto the table, making the glassware rattle. His fingertips pressed together into a two-handed finger gun that bobbed in time with his words. "If it's true, we're gonna have to rip Uncle Sam off the posters and make Susan Chambers the mother of patriots. Congrats, Ms. Chambers. I'm going to make my recommendation that the Department of Defense select Abernathy Ad Executives as their new ad agency."

"Well hot damn, Phil. That *is* good news." Susan tipped her chin down as she lifted the flute of her spritzer. "Cheers to the best decision the US government has made this decade. After the choice to hire you, of course." Susan playfully swiped out, grazing the arm of his jacket, letting an airy little giggle escape. Phil's eyes slid down to the sleeve she just touched and then back up Susan's body. It was slow. It was hungry. It was repulsive. Susan flexed her hand in her lap, methodically opening and closing her fingers. The sensation of her nails leaving little crescent moon craters in her palm calmed her.

"I can't wait to tell Jackie that we're basically going to be working together now!" Jackie was Phil's long-suffering wife—nice enough, but a complete imbecile—and a convenient splash of cold water on the conversation. Susan would've rather swallowed those meaningless brass tacks than be actual friends with the insipid brat, but she wasn't one to leave resources on the table. So, though Susan had done Pilates for years, when the Defense contract was posted and Abernathy himself put Susan in charge of the pitch, she immediately switched studios to the very same studio Phil's wife attended.

Marketing has many angles, and it was Susan's job to play all of them. She could pretend to give a single shit about the troubles of some trophy wife if it allowed her to form a more personal relationship with the man holding those very rich governmental purse strings. It topped having to reverse cowgirl her way into the contract. She'd done it before, but she was getting entirely too old for all that messiness.

Phil pulled himself out of his sexual stupor and straightened once more. His hands went to his tie to tighten the knot. That was his tell. The meeting was over, and he was checking the buckles on his corporate armor before reentering the fray. Susan matched him, running her hands down her lapel. That was not her tell. But she had created it, just for him.

She timed her rise from the table to coincide with his. Then it happened. Phil's hand lifted and extended. It was

The Handshake™. The soft agreement between buddies that was as iron clad as the most legalese-laden document the contracts department could craft.

"You know the gig. I gotta talk to my guys, and there's some finagling with the big birds in Congress, but this bitch is as good as yours, Susan. Congrats, again." Susan grasped his hand and squeezed with everything in her. She loathed getting her hand crushed by self-aggrandizing schmucks but would dish out everything she was given and then some.

"Thank you, Phil. I'll have my girls get you the first draft of the contract so we can start with the redlining while budget is being approved on your end. We're going to revolutionize recruitment together, Phil."

"Stop. You'll get me all hot and bothered with contract talk, Ms. Chambers," Phil purred. Susan batted her eyelashes and ignored the churn of the salad in her belly. "See you in my inbox."

With that, Phil dropped Susan's hand, lifted the breast of his jacket to withdraw his phone, and immediately lifted it to his cheek.

"Curtis, you stuffy bastard. How the hell are you?" Phil shot her a wink and turned, strutting out of the restaurant, loudly continuing to insult Curtis.

As Susan watched Phil walk away, Tad reappeared and slid the check on the table. "I hope the tablecloth helped clinch that handshake deal." Tad muttered. He'd decided to bite back then.

"It didn't do a damn thing to help me. It did annoy you, though. Which means I'll be living rent-free in your head for the afternoon. It's been a good lunch all the way around." Susan didn't break eye contact as she hinged forward to grab her purse from the chair. Sliding the corporate card out of the side pocket, she extended it to him. As the waiter reached out, she let the card slip from her fingers, falling just shy of his hand and clattering on the table. "For me."

A muscle in Tad's jaw twitched. Susan just stared. The contest of wills didn't last long. Tad broke first. His tongue ran along his top lip as he nodded. He swiped the card off the table and shot her one last look of indignation. Moments later he returned, card and receipt in hand. He presented the pair to her silently and bowed his head stiffly when she accepted them. Two men called to heel; it really was a most excellent afternoon.

But she couldn't bask in her own glory for much longer. Even with a word-of-mouth agreement, there was still work to be done. Susan fished her own phone out of her bag and opened her email app. Eighteen emails in the hour and a half she hadn't looked at it. Sixteen of them were from Jim Abernathy asking how the meeting went. The other two were from Jim Abernathy's assistant also asking how the meeting went. Jim Abernathy was at least one hundred and twelve years old and only got involved with the biggest of the big projects at his own firm. And this project that Susan had just secured was the biggest of the biggest.

Tucking her bag under her arm pit, she began pecking out a reply while she walked out of the restaurant. Gliding between the tables, she only kept her periphery focused on not running into things. She absently pulled open the door to Grammercy Tavern and had just stepped out into the crisp, slightly greasy smelling air of the city when she walked straight into the back of a woman just standing in the sidewalk. Susan looked up from her phone to take in the obstacle. It was a middle-aged woman with a fanny pack, glasses too big for her face, and a pretentious neon-colored camera strap looped around her neck, keeping a Nikon suspended at her chest.

"Fucking tourists," Susan spat. "Move." The tourist blinked at her. "Oh, my god, find your self-respect and decency, you insipid, entitled bumpkin. If you must stop, pull to the side so people with actual value can get to where they're going." The woman's mouth fell open, and Susan no longer had any desire to explain sidewalk etiquette. Instead, she put her whole weight into stepping forward, forcing her way past the dimwitted sightseer. Burying herself in her phone, she picked up where she'd left off in the email to her boss.

Jim,

The Eagle has landed. Phil is going to tell his guys to call our guys. We got the fucking contract, Jim. There had better be champagne in that conference room when I get back.

Susan E. Chambers
Senior Vice President
Marketing & Corporate Development
Abernathy Ad Executives
66 Hudson Blvd E
Floor 60
New York, NY 10001

Reviewing her email, pride a swirling vortex in her chest, her thumb moved to the little paper airplane icon on the screen, but just before she managed to hit SEND, screams erupted around her.

Someone in New York is always screaming about something. But these weren't those kinds of screams. No, these were the kind that you paid attention to. They were the tragic, heart-wrenching screams of someone watching something atrocious and disturbing.

Susan Chambers never sent that email.

"**M**s. Chambers? Ms. Chambers…"

Susan's entire body felt like it had been run over by a bus. Everything ached, but her head was pounding most ferociously. She could feel her heartbeat in her eyeballs. A woman's gentle, husky voice called her name again.

"Ms. Chambers. Are you awake?" Even with her eyes still closed, Susan knew the speaker was young. She had a young-sounding voice, still tinged with hope for the future, not yet jaded by the harsh realities that crystalize under the weight of too many years.

"Ms. Chambers…" the voice called again. Yes, this voice definitely belonged to a technical adult, not an actual adult. Actual adults didn't sound perky when trying to wake another adult. Susan tried to speak, but opening her mouth shot a thousand pinpoints of pain across her skull. A wet, gurgling sort of groan escaped her mouth instead of the "leave me alone" she'd been going for.

"Oh! I'm so sorry, Ms. Chambers. Don't try to speak." The voice sounded concerned. "I forgot about the head trauma. Those effects linger. Can you lift your hand for me?"

Head trauma. Did that woman say head trauma? Susan figured that if speaking was hard, opening her eyes would be impossible. Rather than lifting her hand as requested, Susan let it drift across the surface of whatever she was laying on. Soft, fluffy, pleasantly warm. It was a bed. Not a hospital bed. A good one. Hospital beds either feel like plastic or dry loofah sponge. It didn't smell like a hospital either, the lingering cloying sweetness of illness mixed with the burning harshness of bleach and hand sanitizer. No, this room smelled nice. Like old books and apple pie in an old oven. It was comforting and nostalgic. Somehow, it smelled like her grandmother's apartment in the Bronx.

The memory of sitting on her grandmother's bed came rushing back. Susan had spent countless hours of her childhood sitting on that bed, tracing stitches across a patchwork quilt with her finger while she read a book. Those summers in the Bronx were some of Susan's fondest memories, escapes and refuges from her typically busy life at home in Maine. Inhaling deeply through her nose, the smell of pie laced with the faint charred electrical smell of Granny Mae's apartment was exactly right.

Susan tensed. Because it couldn't be exactly right. It was impossible. Granny Mae had been dead for the better part of two decades. The bed, the oven that baked the pies, even the building, had disappeared, torn down and replaced by a different tenement masquerading as livable apartments.

The strange woman's voice interrupted Susan smelling her way to figuring out what the hell was happening. "Very good, Ms. Chambers. I'm going to dim the lights a bit. That typically helps ease the injury response, believe it or not. Let's see if you can open your eyes."

The pinkness of Susan's eyelids faded to a warm crimson, and she cautiously let them open, just a slit, nothing too ambitious. She clenched her butt cheeks in anticipation of the pain, but none came. The world was out of focus, but it was still there, at least. Since opening her eyes the rest of the way didn't hurt, she tried turning her head. Also a painless motion.

She let her head fall toward her left shoulder and sucked in a sharp breath as the fuzz cleared itself up. The nightstand that stared back at her was the nightstand from her childhood, complete with the ballerina lamp, the paper towel tube covered in hair scrunchies, and her necklace of Lip Smackers lip gloss tubes.

"Hello, Ms. Chambers. Welcome. Take a look around. You'll find a lot of interesting things in this room that are going to trigger a lot of memories. That's by design." The woman was somewhere to her right, but Susan couldn't tear her eyes away from that nightstand.

Once upon a time, the table had been a vibrant pink, but when Susan had turned ten, she decided that pink was for babies and convinced her father to buy her black spray paint. Susan had taken that table out to the backyard and spray painted it herself. Poorly. There were drips going all directions somehow, and the black scratched off if she dropped a butterfly clip too aggressively. She'd colored over the peekaboo pink with a sharpie as a teen. Her parents had gleefully dumped it into the annual church yard sale when they converted her old bedroom to a home gym.

And yet there it was. Right there. Drippy, chipped paint job and all.

"How?" That word escaped Susan's lips without her permission.

"Oh, good, welcome. How are you feeling, Ms. Chambers?" The woman spoke with an exuberance Susan found instantly dislikable. She sounded like a nurse, or one of those impossibly patient salesgirls at the makeup counter.

"Like I've been run over by a bus," Susan ground out.

The voice giggled. "Not surprising in the least."

Adrenaline burst through Susan's entire being, burning away the drowsy, foggy veil. She couldn't quite tell if she was angry or afraid, but either way, she bolted upright in bed. "What the hell is happening?" Susan demanded, finally tearing her gaze away from the uncanny table.

"Oh!" The woman squeaked. "Well, feeling much better then. Good." Susan's head whipped toward the voice. The woman couldn't have been over twenty-five, with short bobbed brown hair, a silly micro fringe bang cutting her too-tall forehead in half. Forgettable eyes stared past a nose that was half a size smaller than it should have been. That too-small nose twitched as she smiled sweetly. Susan wanted to dive at her like an angry panther, teeth and claws aimed for the throat. Susan decided she was not afraid. She was angry. Definitely angry.

"Explain everything. Right. Fucking. Now." Susan's kept her voice low, grinding each word between her teeth before she let them past her lips.

"Of course. Would you like a glass of water or—" the woman offered, but Susan cut her off with a roar.

"NOW!"

The smile faded off the woman's face and she nodded, her brown bob tracing zigzags across her cheeks.

"Susan Elizabeth Chambers. You have died." All the anger ebbed immediately. Susan wanted to hold onto that rage, to continue screaming and threatening, but she just wasn't angry anymore. Instead, a foreboding sense of clarity hung itself across Susan's neck, anchoring her in the reality she'd just been presented. The woman continued, "You are currently in what we call the Hall of Memories to begin the experience of your After Death. I am your guide through this process."

"Wait, I'm dead? This is what dead is?"

"Yes. This is what dead is," the guide replied.

"Oh," was all Susan could think to say.

"Damn." The near-adult said, the corner of her mouth pulling to one side in a lopsided expression of disappointment.

"What? Am I not supposed to be dead?" Susan tried and failed to exorcise the wisp of hope from her voice.

"Oh, there isn't really a 'supposed to be' or 'not supposed to be' when it comes to deadness. It's just that you had a 'screamer' vibe. I owe a coworker a soda for it. He said you'd be a 'resigned acceptance.' Which, obviously, you are."

Susan blinked.

The guide continued.

"People take the news that they've died with any of a handful of predictable reactions. Some folks knew what was coming, as they'd been battling a protracted illness. Some folks laugh; that's my favorite reaction." Girl-woman put her hand on her chest and made a sort of sheepish expression. "There's also emphatic relief, angry begging, and finally, screaming, crying, and rending of garments."

At the mention of garments, Susan became aware that she had none. Her tits were swaying in the breeze and the part of her still underneath the quilt was also completely naked. Her hands gently grasped the blanket, tugging it up to her collar bone. The guide noticed Susan notice her naked-ness and immediately spoke, her voice soothing and quiet. "It's okay. There's nothing to be ashamed of. You can be dressed if that makes you more comfortable. Would you like to be dressed?"

Susan only nodded. A tingling feeling skittered up and down her body for the briefest of moments. It felt like someone dropping warmed glitter on her skin. And then she was no longer naked.

Not just no longer naked, but fully clothed, bra and panties and all. Thankfully, no shapewear, given her distinct ability to take a full breath. Susan lifted the hem of the quilt away from her chest and peered down at her own body. She was now wearing her very favorite outfit: a buttery soft pair of deep-sage leggings, great fuzzy grey socks that climbed halfway up her calf, and a storm-grey cable-knit sweater that was at least two sizes too big on her slightly plump frame.

"How?" Once more, that word floated off Susan's lips without her having consciously chosen to say it. Until waking up in this trippy room with nostalgia that was entirely too specific, and now magical emotional-support outfits, Susan would have said she had a way with words. They flowed easily, cutting with the precision of a surgeon when she wanted them to. Susan Chambers was a shark among barracudas in the boardroom. Not only could she sell ice to penguins, Susan Chambers could convince those penguins to forsake their sole habitat and move to the Sahara, were she compensated well enough for her effort.

"We'll get to the how in just a moment. For now, we have some other things to cover, Ms. Chambers."

"Call me Susan." Her words may have abandoned her, but her instinct to befriend before befuddle was still there, even after apparent death.

"Susan. My name is Aurora, and, as I said, I'm your guide through the After Death. You have all the questions and I probably have the answers, but we do need to take it slow. There's a lot to consider and experience and understand, and I promise no one is hiding anything from you or keeping you in the dark. But we've been doing this for a long time—a veritable eternity—and we've learned there are good ways and bad ways to explain what happens after you die. You don't know me from Adam, Eve, or Steve, I am going to have to beg you to trust me."

The whole time she was speaking, Aurora kept her hands raised, palms facing Susan as if she were fending off a bobcat poised to pounce. She spoke quickly and succinctly.

"First things first, let's get the F-A-Q's out of the way." Susan cringed at Aurora spelling out the acronym instead of just saying the words 'Frequently Asked Questions.' The day Susan got her promotion to Senior VP at Abernathy, she sent out a companywide memo saying that the use of acronyms in spoken communiques was absolutely forbidden in Susan's presence. Human Resources had tentatively informed Susan she wasn't allowed to make that a punishable offense. Susan had known that. Nevertheless, the memo worked as intended. No one said stupid stuff like "Oh Em Gee" or "Are Oh Eye" in her presence, if only for fear that she *could* make that offense punishable. If Aurora had noticed the face Susan pulled, she didn't let on.

"No, I am not God. Yes, there is a god. A whole bunch of them. If you'd like to meet one, just let me know at any point and I'll see when they've got an opening on their calendar."

"God has a calendar?" Susan asked blandly.

"They all do, yes. But time doesn't work quite the way you think it does. So yes, they have a calendar, but they can also be at several meetings at the same time." Aurora's lips pressed into a tight line and her brow furrowed in thought. "It's hard to explain just now. But we'll get there. Taking it slow, remember."

Susan nodded as she noticed, for the first time, how put together Aurora was. Her shell blouse was an inviting shade of cream that perfectly paired with the pencil skirt in the same color. A strand of ivory pearls hung at her collarbone and her tall but not towering creamy lace shoes grounded the whole look. It took a particular kind of person to pull off a true monotone palette, and Susan would know. Of the four companies Susan had worked for in her lifetime of marketing, two of them had been fashion industry adjacent.

Susan had barely survived marketing for a mid-size fashion house in the Flat Iron district through the 2016 Monochromatic Movement. Pants, shoes, blazers, bags could be one color of your choice. And only one color. No pops. No accents. If you picked green, you were committing every thread to hue. Susan had gone so far as to make sure even her bra and panties fed the monotony. No one would have been able to accuse her of not living the life she was selling. She was never able to pull it off, though. The fashion industry folks would say it wore her. Aurora, on the other hand, wore that cream on cream on cream like dream.

"What questions do you have for me? What have you always wanted to ask when you died?" Susan's guide asked.

Susan thought for a moment. Of course, she'd vowed that when she died, she'd demand answers to a host of matters both trivial and greatly consequential. Why do bad things happen to good people? Why do children die of cancer? Why does every meat you've never tried apparently taste like chicken?

"Why the mosquitos?" Susan blurted, immediately regretting it. All the questions in the world and she opens with blood-sucking, disease-ridden insects. Aurora let out a knowing giggle.

"You know, that is the second most asked first question," Aurora said matter of factly.

"What's the first most asked first question?" Susan couldn't help herself. She hadn't even gotten the mosquito answer, but now that the question dam had been broken, she wasn't sure she could stem the tide.

"Requests to see a long-lost pet." Aurora replied, a gentle smile appearing through the words. She had subtle parentheses around her mouth—smile lines that were deep and easy. Susan used to have those but had them botoxed to oblivion for her fortieth birthday present to herself. Not for the first time, she idly wondered at the wisdom of all that. Especially since she hadn't even gotten to truly enjoy age-defying skin via botulism, having kicked the damn bucket just two years later.

"Not family members or spouses or loved ones?" Susan fished further.

"Nope. It's dogs, cats, frogs, rats, the occasional ferret or gerbil. Once I even had a lady who raised jumping spiders request to see her very favorite jumping spider, named Parker Peterson. Though, to be fair, the loved ones thing is the third most asked first question. Pets, skeeters, and then people. Humanity can be very predictable in a lot of ways, I suppose." Aurora explained calmly, her hands clasped in front of her hips.

"Interesting." Susan mused. And she was shocked to find that she truly found it interesting. That was one of the words she used when she very much did not find the topic interesting but was stuck in the conversation all the same. "Circling back around to the mosquitos, though." Susan steered the conversation back to her original inquiry.

"Right! Mosquitos were a complete accident. Bill and Herbert are demigods doing their species design internship. They were experimenting with mouth design." Aurora held one hand, palm up. "Bill made a needle mouth." The other hand lifted to match. "Herbert stuck it on a gnat body." She clapped both hands together. "Then they got a little drunk and decided to watch Twilight. Bill thought the idea of a vampire bug was hilarious. Herbert agreed and suggested they make it smart like Carlisle, moody like Edward, and defiantly stubborn like Rosalie."

Aurora's face stayed brilliantly neutral through all of this. Susan knew her own face was stuck somewhere between shock and confusion. She didn't bother to fix that as Aurora plowed on.

"They took that needle-mouth gnat and made it vampiric, smart, moody, and stubborn. If you look closely, mosquitoes glitter in the sun. But their bodies are just so small, so you really don't notice the sparkle. Anyway, Bill and

Herbert got the rest of the way drunk and passed out without having contained the glitter vampire bug properly. It got out and bred with other gnats and it's been a problem ever since." Aurora's hands found her hips and perched there. "Every time we think we have a solution, the bug uses those smarts Bill and Herbert gave it and outsmarts all our extinction level events. We went big with the whole global flood thing and the bastards learned to breed in water."

Susan stared. She blinked. She stared some more. No matter how she turned it over in her mind, the story didn't make sense. Tentatively, she tried repeating it, as if saying it out loud would somehow help. "I just want to confirm some things. Twilight, the teeny-bopper movie with angsty, glittery vampires predates mosquitos? And said mosquito, somehow younger than a movie that was released in 2009, was created by two drunk guys named Bill and Herbert. Is that right?"

Aurora had the sense to look slightly abashed. "Yes, and also no. Remember, time works differently than you suppose. All the timelines are separate and simultaneous." She paused, chewing on her lower lip. "I know it's a lot to take in. Twilight came out in 2009 in your timeline, but it's also always existed. You just had to know where to look to find it while in control of your own temporal speed." Susan's face must have looked even more confused, as Aurora added, "Which most people aren't, and for good reason. But yeah, you've got the gist of it. Drunk demigods made a Twilight-inspired murder bug."

"Okay. Okay, wait." Susan said. "I think I understand what's happening." Aurora lifted her eyebrows toward her micro-fringe bangs and waited for Susan to continue. "Who did it?" Aurora's eyes darted to and fro, seeking context.

"Who did what?" she asked politely.

"Who drugged me? Was it Alana? She's had an itchy ass about my promotion to Senior VP for three years, and that woman can hold a grudge. Did she, like, triple my shroom microdose? Drop some MDMA on my keyboard or something? Did she roofie my greens shake and I'm lying in the gym bathroom hallucinating right now?"

Then Susan realized how inane she was being. Of course, the hallucination couldn't explain itself to her. Not knowing what else to do, she pinched her arm. It hurt, but she stayed, ass snuggled down in a bed that looked like her grandmother's next to an incredibly nostalgic nightstand. No sudden waking. No reentry of reality.

"That's a very common reaction. You can continue to try to stimulate your pain response if you'd like, but all that going to do is make you sore. You're not dreaming or seizing or hallucinating. You're dead. And that's not a bad thing, Susan."

"See, that is exactly what I would think a drug-induced hallucination would say." Susan smacked herself hard across the face. Harder than she thought she should have been able to smack herself. Pain erupted across her occipital and she thought her eyeball might have exploded in the socket. The non-slapping hand immediately rose to cradle her fiery cheek. Susan opened and closed her mouth to see if she'd dislocated her own jaw. That should not have hurt as much as it did. Aurora watched calmly, but Susan was starting to get a little short of breath. The panic in her chest began to rise.

If this was real, then she'd been kidnapped. Was this step one in getting sex trafficked? Susan tried to force herself to breathe like a regular human, slow and steady. If she was kidnapped, should she try to escape or wait for her friends and family to find that she was missing? Would the police intervene? Did she want a big, dramatic SWAT raid, busting down the door? She was now panting like an overtired dog, though as she reckoned with how long it might take for someone to call the police. Or even notice she was missing.

Her friends, while wonderful, were quite accustomed to Susan disappearing into a "work mode" for days, weeks, even months. Unanswered texts and being left on read were the norm when it came to being friends with Susan Chambers.

She'd been married once. To Kevin. Who had been just as married to his job as she was to hers. When Susan caught

Kevin bonking his fourth coworker, this one named John, Susan hadn't been terribly reluctant to hand him those divorce papers. Quite honestly, she'd been relieved. They'd argued about nothing, divided up their stuff, and the divorce was smooth as a dolphin's ass. Kevin would not notice that his ex had disappeared at this point.

Susan's parents were dead, and she hadn't bothered speaking to them for years before they were pushing up daisies anyway.

Her boss, Jim Abernathy, might be mildly annoyed to not hear from her, but she wasn't totally sure Jim Abernathy even knew what she looked like, much less if she was or was not in the office. He was more of a "big-picture guy" than the type to remember that the people who worked for him were people, rather than very life-like automatons.

As Susan's eyes fell back to Aurora, she was transformed into the enemy, though her demeanor did not suggest she'd noticed. She did, however, seem to develop a sud-den knack for telepathy.

"You've not been kidnapped. You're not in danger. You are free to leave this room and wander, explore, experience as much as you'd like. No one is keeping you here, and no one will tell you not to be somewhere or to do something."

"I could snap your neck and run into the street, and no one would say boo?" Susan challenged, a defiant edge turning her voice more toward petulance than dominance, much to Susan's chagrin.

"Exactly. Although, I sincerely hope you skip the neck-snapping part." Aurora replied, still annoyingly unperturbed. "And there are no streets. Just this building. But it's a really big building. Like, you cannot comprehend how big this building is. But you can explore every inch of it, if you'd like."

Susan flung the blanket off and swung her socked feet to the floor. As her feet hit the carpet, she noticed a pair of crystal-white Keds sitting on the floor, the heel boxes collapsed from years of being wiggled onto her feet without bothering to untie the laces. She hesitated. Those were her favorite Keds; a pale purple splotch on the toe of the left one gave it away.

Four days after she bought them, she'd dripped a globule of Heather Hustle nail polish on them. Despite bi-weekly bleaching, nothing would touch that damn blob of Sally Hansen's Insta-Dry. Muscle memory slid her feet into the Keds.

Susan had been wearing her precious and prized Manolo Blahniks, vibrant orange, to complement her lucky powder-blue power suit. But those shoes, the suit, her purse were nowhere. Susan examined the room more thoroughly. It was just a room, non-descript bordering on sterile, grey-beige walls, pale-honey floors. The bed had been transported from her grandmother's house. The shoes had come from her closet. The nightstand from her girlhood bedroom.

Susan tried to remember exactly what happened before she'd awoken next to a wild collection of impossibly specific nostalgia. There was a divine Caesar salad, the handshake, that snippy waiter, the tourist on the sidewalk, and then screaming. And screeching. And then nothing. Absolutely nothing. The more Susan tried to focus on that gap in her memory, the more nothing it became, solidifying and taking a form that refused to be defined or understood.

Susan's head had stopped pounding, but it still swam. She couldn't manage more than a whisper but said, "You think I'm dead?" She flicked her eyes to Aurora, who had not changed position this whole time. She stood straight and tall between two doors across the room from where Susan still perched in the bed. Her hands were still clasped before her.

"I know you're dead, Susan. You know you're dead."

Susan let the silence settle around her, feeling the weight of it pull her into enlightenment. She was dead. Really, truly dead. The room was oppressively silent. "How did I die?" Susan croaked, the quiet shattering around her words. Aurora started just a bit, her hand finally breaking rank and flying to her mouth to stifle either a gag or a giggle, Susan couldn't tell which.

"Okay, of all the things I expect you not to believe, this might top the pile…" Aurora paused, and her gaze floated upward as if she were searching for the right words somewhere on the ceiling. "You died by getting hit by a bus."

"Stop." Susan replied, the gravity of the situation that had threatened to hold her hostage burned away with the inanity of how she died. She felt her head fall to the side, a vague gesture of indignant disbelief.

"You didn't. Stop, that is. You were writing an email on your phone and stepped off the curb right into the path of a bus. The bike rack caught you right here"—Aurora turned and showed the back of her head, dropping her chin to her chest and using her index finger to point to that soft part at the bottom of the skull where it joins your neck—"right at the brain stem. You were gone before you realized what happened. Which is why you can't remember dying."

"Wait, do most people remember their own death?" Susan was incredulous.

"Some do if they expected the dying. Most don't. The human brain does a lot of things to protect itself and its body when in crisis. And dying is a bit of a crisis, according to the brain. It stops dumping information in the short term while its busy trying not to die. With no short-term memory, there is nothing to commit to mid-term or long-term memory." Aurora rocked up on her toes and lowered slowly back down. It was somehow a comforting motion to watch. "So no, most people do not remember their death. Though, a few unlucky folks do remember the incident that led to their death, especially if medical assistance was provided and they spent some time semi-cognizant during life-saving treatment."

Susan was very grateful she did not remember being hit by a bus.

"Is that why everything hurt when I woke up? Because I was waking up from being hit by a bus?" Susan's stomach clenched and if she'd had anything in it, she had the distinct impression she'd have a second opportunity to see it.

"Yes, in a way. When you wake up," Aurora used finger quotes to emphasize 'wake up,' "you still retain a kind of snapshot of the sensation you were experiencing the moment your body ceased to function. You weren't actually in pain lying in this bed. It was more the memory of pain that once was. You only experience pain if you think you're supposed to feel pain, prompted by environmental stimuli. Technically, you don't have a body now, so you don't have nerve endings or a brain to transmit pain."

Susan looked down at her very real-feeling body. Aurora beamed as she elaborated. "I know it looks like you are in a body, but it's an illusion. You currently exist in your very basest form; you might call this version of existence your soul. Or your consciousness. Or your life force."

Susan's eyebrows scrunched themselves closer together as puzzle pieces slid into place. "Then why do I see and feel a body? Why did it feel like I pulverized my own skull when I slapped myself?" she challenged.

"Because it makes you feel better to see yourself in a body. Your soul or awareness has seen itself in a body for the greater part of its existence. When it is removed from a body, say by having that body smashed, dragged, and decimated by the undercarriage of a bus, it still thinks of itself as having one. You perceive yourself in corporeal form because that's known and safe territory. But your soul isn't normally in charge of an entire nervous system, so it approximates what pain should feel like. Which means some things hurt less than they ought to, and some things hurt more."

"That's why it hurt so much when I slapped myself," Susan felt a grin tug at her lips as understanding dawned. Aurora nodded with enthusiasm.

"Yes. Exactly. In corporeal form, it hurts if you slap yourself. But your soul can only guess how much that action should hurt. You can regulate that. If you don't want to feel pain, you simply decide not to feel any. If you want to be cold, you can choose to feel cold. You even choose how to present yourself. That's why when you decided to be dressed, your clothes appeared."

"I did that? I thought about being clothed and then my clothes just manifested on my body that isn't a body?"

"Exactly!" Aurora sounded chipper. It grated on Susan's apparently imaginary nerves.

"If I wanted to appear as a cat, could I do that?"

"Maybe." Aurora replied. "It depends on whether you can truly see yourself as a cat. It goes a little deeper than just picturing a cat in your mind's eye and putting yourself inside it. You must be able to wrap your mind around everything it would take for you to be a cat. From having a tail to grooming your butthole with your tongue." Susan's face betrayed her disgust. Aurora scrunched her nose up in solidarity. "It's gross to consider that, but if you can fully reconcile every human instinct to the equivalent feline instinct, then yes, you could appear as cat. Your soul won't care. In fact, it's probably been a cat before."

Aurora held a manicured finger up for a moment and her eyes drifted back toward the ceiling again. "Yep. Your soul has been a cat before."

Susan realized her mouth was hanging open and she snapped it shut. "My soul has been a what now?" Aurora's serene mask slipped just a bit and her lips pulled back to reveal shame-clenched teeth.

"I probably shouldn't have mentioned that just yet, but now that the cat's literally out of the bag, yes; your soul has been a cat before. It's also been all the genders and several other species."

"Reincarnation. You're talking about reincarnation."

"That's one word for it, yes. We call it 'cycling' around these parts, but reincarnation is as good a term as any. In a very simplified nutshell, souls do have a finite lifespan, but it is significantly longer than most forms of physical life." Aurora was unnaturally still. It almost gave Susan that uncanny feeling that looking at one of those animatronic faces might have. Almost.

"What is a soul?" Susan asked, but she knew that wasn't the right question. She tried again. "Explain to me like I'm five what a soul is made up of."

Aurora's eyes drifted upward, likely looking for the best way to approach such a heady question. She took a deep breath, focused on Susan again, and began.

"A soul isn't a physical thing in that it doesn't take up space or require sustenance like food or water to live. A soul is energy in its purest form. It's why you can change your appearance by deciding to do so. Here, in this realm or version of existence, you are just energy coalesced into a form that feels familiar and safe." Susan looked down at her body again, desperately trying to match Aurora's words to Susan feeling like she had a body. It almost wanted to make sense. Aurora continued. "Your soul did not die when your body ceased functioning via bus. After that body could no longer house the soul, your soul instinctively returned here, to the space between life and death. Arrangements can now be made for a new physical form to house your soul. Once one lifespan is completed, your soul cycles to another form to live out that lifespan. This pattern will repeat until the soul itself has worn away and eventually fades out of existence."

"How long does that take, normally?" Susan asked. She felt like a child being told a bedtime story.

"Mileage may vary. In temporal terms you're familiar with, a soul typically exists for two to three quadrillion years, give or take a trillion or so." Aurora faced her palms upward and wobbled back and forth like a scale trying to find its balance.

"I'm sorry. Could you run those numbers by me one more time?" Susan asked, not even bothering to hide the disbelief in her voice.

"A soul typically exists for two to three quadrillion Earth years." Aurora returned with a curt nod. "Give or take a trillion."

"Not to be a stickler, or to pretend I know more than a guide to the…" Susan searched her lap for the words but came up empty. "What did you call it again?"

"The After Death," Aurora supplied.

"I'm sure I don't know more than a guide to the After Death. But I don't think the universe is that old. How could you know that's how long a soul exists?"

"That is a most excellent question, Susan." Aurora said, sounding only a little bit like a kindergarten teacher. "The universe as you understand it is only 13.7 billion years old, according to your math." Aurora assessed Susan for a moment. Susan stared back before gesturing for her guide to continue. "Remember, time is weird, and doesn't work the way you think it does. No one has yet to properly demonstrate how time works to the general human population of twenty-first-century Earth. Russell T. Davies was so close to explaining it, but he chose a television show to try to educate the masses about temporal physics and everyone thought that it was just silliness and campy special effects."

"Russell T.… *Doctor Who*. Russel T. Davies was the show runner for *Doctor Who*." Susan wasn't sure why she'd retained that obscure trivia. "You're saying that's real? That math is wrong. That the universe is older than we think and that *Doctor Who* is a real thing?

"Oh, no." Aurora giggled. It was an airy, effeminate sound. "*Doctor Who* is completely made up. No such thing as Daleks, Gallifrey, or TARDISes. But the temporal physics addressed: those were very, very real. It's kind of like when you tell kids a story about a tortoise and a hare. At the end you get this whole lesson about perseverance and pride, right? Well *Doctor Who* was a nice, easy-to-watch story that was trying to educate humanity about how time works. Unfortunately, Davies was a gifted storyteller, and the lesson he was trying to teach sort of got lost in the narrative." At this, Aurora shrugged, her lips pressed in a tight, disappointed line.

"People assume that time is a strict progression of cause to effect, but actually, from a nonlinear, non-subjective viewpoint, it's more like a big ball of wibbly-wobbly, timey-wimey… stuff." Susan quoted the only line from she remembered from the show.

"You're a *Doctor Who* fan?" Aurora leaned forward, her hair falling in curtains around her face. She seemed genuinely shocked for the first time since Susan woke up in the After Death.

"No. Definitely not. I'm more a *Desperate Housewives*, *Sex and The City* gal. No, my assistant loved that sort of shit and had that quote cross-stitched and framed in her cubicle."

"Oh. Fair enough. And yes. That's completely correct. Time is not linear, but it is cyclical. Every point in history can be connected to every other point in history with very little effort by just folding them together and pushing away the bits that want to get in the way while making the fold. Navigating history and time is sort of like folding a fitted sheet. Once you know the trick of tucking the corners together and creating a fake corner beside the real corner, it works every time. But it's incredibly finicky to master and not always worth the effort." Aurora's expression was one of patience and understanding. Susan knew hers was of horror and confusion.

"Can you manipulate time?" Susan cautiously asked.

"Yes." Aurora's answer was clipped but not angry.

"Can I manipulate time?" She ventured a question, quite sure she knew the answer.

"At current, no. But you can learn, if you're interested. It sort of depends on what you'd like to do next."

"I'd like to return to a place where sane conversation happens."

"Believe it or not, this *is* sane conversation. But we are moving pretty fast. I'm going to try again to go a little slower. I don't want to overwhelm you, and I fear we're getting perilously close to that threshold." Aurora's face brightened as Susan's crumpled. "Let's take a walk. We have plenty of things that will help you make sense of everything. This is going to be a great first day for both of us."

"First day?" Susan sputtered. "This is your first day on the job?"

"Yes and no." Aurora stated with no shame in her voice.

"Do you *ever* give a straight answer?"

"Yes." Aurora said. Susan raised an eyebrow and waited. "And no." Aurora broke eye contact with her and frowned sheepishly. "I give straight answers as you are able to grapple with them. The more time we spend together, the less it will feel like I'm dodging questions."

"So how is this both your first day and not?"

"You are the first soul I'm guiding through the After Death by myself. I've shadowed other guides and had other guides shadow me. But you are the first soul I am guiding alone. Of course, I have support and a fantastic team behind me, but there is no one waiting in the wings to swoop in in case of error."

"Error? What kind of errors?"

"Sharing too much too quickly can sort of cause a soul to go into safety mode. Think of 'limp mode' in a car. If we dump all the information about the space between physical forms without laying the proper groundwork, a soul can panic a little bit, and it takes forever to get it to calm back down. But don't worry." Aurora's hands were back in the 'calm a pred-ator' position again, palms up and pressed toward Susan. "I think we're past that hurdle. You've already onboarded a lot and you're hanging in there just fine!" Again, the false perkiness sprinkled in the spaces between her words was just a little bit irksome to Susan.

"How many souls did you help with before going solo with mine?"

Aurora started counting on her fingers. "Um…" a few more finger taps. "372"

"Oh. Okay. That's quite a—" Susan was going to say 'few' until Aurora continued.

"Thousand."

"Damn." Susan said, her shock overriding her filter. Before she could stop herself, she asked, "How old are you?"

"Old enough to have helped with that many souls. Remember, time—"

"Works differently than I think." Susan finished for her. "Yeah. That bit is beginning to sink in, I think." Something occurred to Susan. "So if I'm not in a body, instead just a visual representation of one, are you in a body?"

"Yes." Aurora replied. Susan waited. Again. "And no." Susan's hand flew over her head, exasperated. "I am in a body, but not this one. My real body is in a completely different space, and I am interfacing with the energy that comprises your soul. My voice is mine, but my face, my body, my clothes—these were all specifically chosen to help you feel comfortable and safe. Sometimes, guides end up in the form of loved ones, former bosses or mentors, or total strangers. In your case, it's a total stranger. About that walk, though; let's go stroll down memory lane, eh?"

"You said there were no streets here," Susan offered, knowing it was petty and not really caring.

"Well, no. Not a literal lane." Susan noted the frustration that flickered across her guide's face, but it was gone in an instant. Aurora corrected course. "I meant figuratively. Your memories are an important part of your experience and revisiting the fondest ones often helps the soul release one form to choose another." As she spoke, Aurora opened the door to her left and waved an arm to allow Susan through first.

As Susan stepped through, she asked, "Choose another form? You mean I'm going to choose what my next life is?" Susan wasn't sure why that made her feel odd.

"Exactly," came Aurora's reply. They were now standing in a long hall. It reminded her of a hotel hallway. Or it would have if there were any other doors along the walls. There were none; just the occasional sconce with a light bulb that was shaped to look like a flame.

The walls were a pleasing taupe color, and the carpet was a deep emerald-green. Susan had always wanted emerald-green carpet but always talked herself out of it. Too dated, she'd thought. If only she'd known that time worked different. She might have sprung for the green floor.

"Right now, you're convinced that you are *simply* Susan Chambers, born in Bangor, Maine and a resident of New York City since 1999 when you moved there to attend NYU." She sounded like a tour guide on one of those obnoxious double-decker busses.

"And that's not true?" Susan challenged.

"It is, but that's not the only truth. You are Susan Chambers of Manhattan by way of Bangor. But that's not all you are. You've lived in many forms prior to this one, including as a cat, and you are quite a young soul. You'll have many more forms after this next one. All those experiences make you who you are. Your past lives inform the decisions your soul makes in future iterations of itself."

"But if I've lived other lives already, I don't remember them. And all the people who swear up and down they *do* remember their past lives are always loony tunes." Susan swirled her finger in a tight circle near her temple for emphasis.

Aurora's lips pursed, a hint of disappointment flavoring her tone. "They aren't loony tunes." The disapproval hung on every syllable, the way she said it. "But most of them are lying. At least the ones who provide details. Occasionally, some things do leak into the next form a soul takes. Most of the time, you experience these leaks as a feeling of de ja vu, or that sensation you get when you think you saw someone you knew but when you looked again it wasn't them."

"If we don't remember our past lives, how are decisions shaped by them?"

"Because your soul has gained experience. Ever met someone who was wise beyond their years?" Susan's brows pulled together as she considered. "As in, they had a clarity about them and a way of viewing the world and its problems that felt out of synch with their age?" Aurora elaborated. She had met several folks like that. Susan let her chin dip once. "A lot of times, you'd call that person an 'old soul.' Well, it's likely they *are* an old soul. They've had a lot of experience and time to consider how best to approach a problem, and they make solid decisions as a result, even if the corporeal form they are in seems too young to be capable of that sort of insight. The body is young, but the soul is experienced and wizened."

Susan sat with that. She had met several people too smart for their age. Sometimes too smart for their own good. Her own niece, Mikayla, her brother Samuel's youngest daughter, was among them. As an infant, Mikayla had screamed and cried and shat her pants like every other baby. But the child also had a way of considering you that was unnerving. She wasn't just looking *at* you; she was look-ing *in* you.

As she got older, those surreal moments never really stopped. She'd say the most bizarrely poignant things. Once, when Susan was visiting her brother Samuel and his kids in Chicago, Mikayla discovered Susan in the kitchen, pouring herself a cup of coffee. Samuel and his wife had left their three kids in Susan's care to enjoy a day on the town.

The then-eight-year-old Mikayla asked if Susan could help her make a cup of hot cocoa. Susan had told her she'd have to ask Samuel about that. Without missing a beat, Mikayla had responded, "You could ask Daddy if I can have cocoa. But you don't have to. Because I can. I have a body that can drink cocoa, and we have cocoa and hot water here. So yes, I can have hot cocoa. You could ask my dad if I *should* have hot cocoa." Mikayla blazed through the words like it hurt her to keep them inside her mind. Leaving almost no air between her words, Susan's niece powered on with her justification for not calling her father about cocoa. "But we don't have to ask him that, either, because last night, at bedtime, Daddy told me to be safe and have fun today. Asking my Aunt Susan for hot cocoa is safe because of the hot water and fun because of the hot cocoa. I'm doing exactly what Daddy told me to do. I don't think we have to ask him because I think he already told me it was okay." Susan couldn't argue the point, so she made the kid a hot cocoa.

"Mikayla. My niece. She is an old soul in a child's body." Once more, Aurora's eyes drifted skyward before darting back down to Susan's face.

"Yes. She is. That soul is very old. Probably nearing the end of its existence."

"Why do you do that?" Susan asked.

"Do what?" Aurora asked, genuinely curious.

"Sometimes your eyes just roll upward and then you come back."

Aurora snickered. "Oh, that's what happens when I look something up. Remember, I have a real body. And that real body is sitting at a computer terminal with what looks kind of like a VR headset on my face. I can see and interact with everything in this room through that interface. It also tracks my movements, so you see me moving naturally, as if I were truly in the room with you." Aurora turned her head in demonstration. "But I also see a bunch of heads-up displays. Some energy readings that help me guess how you're about to react. Some data about the life you just experienced and some search windows of general knowledge to help me best explain what you're currently experiencing. When I look up at those extra windows, you see my eyes drift upward, because real-me is looking up as well."

"Time is not linear, and you can control it, but you're using a VR headset to talk to me? There isn't a better interface system available somewhere in the annals of time?"

Aurora sort of bobbed her head as if she were trying to decide how best to answer. She opened her mouth to say something, but Susan interjected, "If you say 'yes… and no,'" Susan lifted her voice in a decent mimicry of Aurora's, "I'm going to give you quite an energy reading to make sense of." Aurora closed her mouth. She was silent for a heartbeat and then opened her mouth again.

"Well, first, human technology really takes a nosedive in the twenty-second century. And second, there are a variety of interfaces available to those of us who serve as guides. We choose the tools we prefer. I prefer the twenty-first century style interfaces. There's one girl who uses nanobots—very 'Marvel Cinematic Universe, Tony Stark, and too much CGI' vibes. And there's another guy who uses this big tactile interface thing. Ever seen the movie *Minority Report?*"

"Yes?" Susan replied.

"That. Pretty much. A few minor modifications to make it work, but his workstation looks like that touch, swipe, gesture, screen-floaty thing like in *Minority Report.*"

"How did you get this job?"

"I chose it."

"You can just choose to do this?"

"Yes, at a certain point, you can choose to guide other souls through their After Death."

"Can I choose that?"

"You, as you are now: no. Your soul is too young to do this work just yet. But at some point, yes, you will be able to choose to do this work. And you'd get to choose your own workstation and interface, too," Aurora explained easily.

"My soul is too young? How old is my soul?" Something in Susan wanted to be just a little offended at being too young for something. It had been a lot of years since she was too young for anything. Before the bus incident, she'd begun to discover she was too old for a few things, but too young felt irritating. Aurora's eyes lifted again.

"2.3 trillion years old."

"And that's young?" Susan was having trouble with this new extreme math she was learning. She couldn't reasonably envision what a million of something was, much less a billion or 2.3 trillion.

"Yeah." Aurora's head bobbed in long, exaggerated nods. "It's practically a newborn." Aurora had started meandering down this long, doorless hall as they'd talked. She seemed to have a destination in mind.

"Are new souls born?" Susan found that while she had never once considered the metaphysics of souls, it was a fascinating thing to think about, now that it had occurred to her to think about it.

"Yes. A new soul is born every time a star collapses. That's what you would call a black hole. That weird phenomenon where it seems like matter and light and anti-matter and true dark collide is the exact point in time and space where a new soul comes into existence."

"You're saying that stars are soul embryos?"

"I'd say fetus is a more apt descriptor, but yes. Pretty much. That's a good way to look at it, from a human perspective."

"And if a star is, say, blown up, *Star Wars*-style—that's like a soul abortion?"

"If a star could be blown up, yes, that would be correct. But so far, no one has attempted to blow up a star, to the best of my knowledge. Because, honestly, what would be the point? It's a star, a burning ball of gas and matter floating in space, sometimes with its own planetary system hovering around it."

"Are there other planets with people on them elsewhere in the universe?" Susan asked, remembering that she had free reign to ask all the questions she'd ever wondered about.

"There are planets with other lifeforms. Lots and lots of them. Not all of them are what you would call people. There is one planet in our universe that is inhabited by sentient trees. They look and act and function exactly like trees on Earth, except they are alive and very aware of what's happening to them and around them. There's another planet inhabited by beings that are made of congealed light."

"Congealed? Did you describe light as congealed? Like…" Susan cast about for the right word. "Like Jell-O? There's a planet of Jell-O… Flashlights?"

"I wouldn't call them that to their facial orifice, but yes, Jell-O flashlights is one way to describe them." Aurora was

clearly stifling a chuckle at that. "And then there is everything beyond your known universe."

"Beyond my known universe? What does that mean?"
Susan had apparently mastered suspension of disbelief, a
thing she wasn't very good at in life. Or her most recent
life, anyway. No one would watch movies with Susan
Chambers because Susan couldn't help herself from
pointing out every single mistake, continuity error, his-
torical inaccuracy, or break in the laws of physics, chem-
istry, or biology. It was the same with books and art. If
there was something that belied its existence as a made
up or created thing, Susan would spot and call attention
to it. As a child, she never even wanted to go to the most
magical place on earth. It wasn't magical; it was man
made. And as such, it was little more than a giant fishing
net for catching the gullible and all the money in their
wallets.

"Time being time as you're coming to understand it means
that beyond the known universe is the multi-verse. Or the
strings, the strands, the alternate realities."

"You mean somewhere out there is a world where Susan
Chambers did not get run over by a bus?"

"Yes. There is a world where Susan Chambers did not get
run over by a bus. Several, actually."

"Okay, then we can skip the memory lane and be done
with all this. If I get to choose where I go, then I want to be

the Susan Chambers who did not get run over by a bus." Aurora nodded, but she had this little line between her eyebrows as she did. Susan knew that line meant she was about to say something regretful.

"That Susan Chambers is already spoken for. Another soul is experiencing that version of Susan Chambers. And another soul is experiencing the Susan Chambers who quit her job to be an actress. And yet another soul has already experienced the Susan Chambers who died of influenza when she was seven."

Susan gasped. "I had a terrible case of influenza when I was seven. *I* almost died. I was in the hospital for weeks. I still carry an inhaler because of the damage it did to my lungs. Well, carried, I guess. Did all the Susan Chambers' have that flu?"

"No, not all of them. But a good chunk of them did have influenza when they were seven," Aurora intoned.

"So that's how souls live for quadrillions of years. It's not that they're older than the universe. It's that they can experience layers and layers of the same universe and all its variations?"

"That's a very simple explanation of a deeply complicated concept, but yeah, that's the basic basics of it." A sort of proud smirk was trying to inch its way across Aurora's face. It was then that Susan could take no more of the endless, doorless hallway.

"Where are we going, by the way?" Susan inquired, though she'd sounded more impatient than she'd meant to.

"Oh, that's up to you. This is the hall of memories. You have an opportunity to relive any moment your soul experienced this go-round. Anything you want to see again, moments you'd like to reexperience, things you'd like to go back and see if what you remember is what really happened. You get to choose what parts of this life you'd like to revisit."

"Why would I want to do that?"

Aurora shrugged. "Some people don't. Some people were happy with their memories and didn't want to see how badly they misremembered something. Some folks want a replay of their whole life."

"Wouldn't that take an entire life to relive?"

"It does. But time…" Susan waved a hand through the air as if trying to brush away what Aurora was going to say next. Aurora nodded and did not complete the sentence. "Is there any moment you want to see?"

"What about things I don't remember? Can I see that?"

"If you were present for it, yes. I can't make memories that don't exist. For instance, I can't take you back to watch Lincoln's Gettysburg address because Susan Chambers was not present for the Gettysburg address. But if you were there, even if you don't actively remember it, I can show you that memory with one exception."

"What's the exception?"

"At this moment, I cannot show you the moment of your death. First, it is often deeply upsetting for people who experienced a traumatic death; and second, those memories are very damaged and disjointed because of your body's loss of function in that moment."

"My brain got bus-pancaked before I remembered anything?" Susan offered.

"Your brain got bus-pancaked, yeah." Aurora returned. Susan stared at the blob of polish on her shoe while she considered. What would she want to relive? Susan had not been much for nostalgia. Sure, there were a few sentimental items she toted around with her; a few pictures of her brother's family, a few mementos from college high points. Suddenly, it occurred to her what she wanted to see.

"Can I see if Alexis Johnson actually stole that lipstick from my middle-school makeup shop?" Susan's voice betrayed her excitement. It had bugged her that she was never sure of what happened to that damn lipstick.

Susan's mother had been incredibly strict, but she also celebrated being a "proper lady" above everything else. While Susan had not been allowed to watch television because it would rot her brain, her mother had taught her to do a full face of makeup by the time Susan turned ten. By the time the rest of Susan's peers were finally allowed to play in their own piles of fancy, dirty, tinted goo, Susan was miles ahead of them. Seeing an opportunity to capitalize on her skills and privilege, she opened her own makeup stand.

Some kids had lemonade stands or paper routes. Susan Chambers had herself a middle school makeup counter outside her middle school Home Economics room. For a quarter per color, Susan would expertly paint her friends' faces for them. A swipe of frosty blue shadow, a smear of obnoxiously pink lipstick, a poof of blush and everyone walked away satisfied.

Alexis Johnson was one year older than Susan, one of Susan's regulars from the eighth grade. Alexis dutifully reported for her makeover every day before school. One such morning, Susan looked down to realize her tube of Cover Girl Precious Plum had gone missing, the very same Precious Plum that Alexis Johnson chose every single time.

Alexis had even asked Susan not to use that color on anyone else. "Everyone has a signature color, and Precious Plum is mine, you see." Susan had seen, but she knew it would be bad for business. There was a gaggle of seventh graders that only paid for lipstick, and all chose Precious Plum.

Susan knew this was something she should have let go years ago, but she knew deep in her very bones that Alexis had taken that lipstick. It was silly, but Susan was excited to finally lay this makeup mystery to rest.

"Absolutely. Excellent choice." Aurora stepped to the side, and behind where she'd been standing was a door. Susan knew full well that door had not been there a moment ago, but given all the other things she'd experienced in this last… however long she'd been wherever she was now… knew it wasn't worth trying to make sense of.

"Now, before you enter, I need to prepare you for what you're going to experience. When you open this door you will see, hear, feel, smell, and taste everything you did at the time. You will have no control over what's happening, as this is a memory. Kind of like being a passenger in a car you're not driving. I'll be able to hear and understand your thoughts, but you won't be able to see me, and I won't be able to respond. This representation," Aurora gestured down at her form "will not enter memories with you, but I'll still be right there. If at any point you wish to stop revisiting the memory, we need to establish a safe word. Say, or rather think, the word and the memory will stop. You'll return here."

"Aardvark." Susan stated with confidence.

"Aardvark?" Aurora double-checked.

"Aardvark. When, in regular conversation, does someone use the word aardvark? That's a very intentional word choice. It can't be anything other than a safe word." Susan explained. Her twenties had really been something.

"Fair enough. Aardvark it is. If you want out, simply think the word 'aardvark' and the memory will end. Ready?"

"I guess. Yeah?" Susan wasn't sure what sort of mental preparation she should be engaging in.

"Alright. Open the door and the memory will take over."

Susan opened the door, and that tingling sensation swept over her body. It felt like when your foot has fallen asleep and a million pins go digging around in your flesh. It was uncomfortable and verging on pain, but not quite there. Then the sensation was gone, and Susan was stood in the hallway of her middle school.

Her stomach was gnawing on itself. That had been a staple of Susan's middle school experience. She was always hungry because she was always skipping meals. Not too many, but enough that her mother wouldn't be tempted to make her go back to daily weigh-ins. Susan also felt greasy. Every bit of her felt slightly oily. She did not miss puberty even a little bit.

"Susan!" Susan's head turned of its own volition, and she was briefly surprised. It was disorienting to feel her head turn without having chosen to turn it. She was reminded that she was merely a passenger in this memory when a very young voice came out of her mouth.

"Alexis! Here for your daily look?"

"Of course. Of course." Alexis Johnson was the epitome of an upper-middle-class middle schooler. Several tank tops were layered over another, the lacy edges pulled down past the low-rise hips of her flared jeans. The bright-white toes of Adidas tennis shoes peaked out from under the slightly frayed denim hems. That day, Alexis had woven a basket pattern across the top of her skull with twists of hair and miniature rainbow rubber bands.

She jogged toward Susan's setup, the collection of ball-chain necklaces and enameled pendants around Alexis' neck jangling. Alexis let her backpack slide off her shoulder, the pins rattling as it hit the floor beside the slightly wobbly desk Susan had commandeered as her workstation.

"Any mascara today?" Alexis sounded wistful. She asked every day, and every day Susan had to say no. To share her mascara, she'd need more spoolie brushes. That would involve asking her parents, and Susan knew if her mother figured out she was whoring herself out as a makeup artist, the whole business plan would go up in flames. Susan quite enjoyed her pocket money. She figured she'd have to convince her father to take her to the mall while he was home next weekend. She'd snag a few from the Clinique counter.

"No. Not today." Susan apologized. Alexis pouted until Susan added, "But I got a new eyeshadow. It's white and super shimmery. And!" Susan's finger stabbed the air before she dove into her backpack. "Cucumber Melon spray is back!"

Susan finished most of her looks off with a spritz or two of her coveted Bath & Body Works body spray, but she'd exhausted her supply a couple days ago. Susan had endured her mother's lecture that she'd been using entirely too much perfume. 'A lady's scent should be subtle and fresh; not like we bathed in a smoothie.' Susan must have looked just sorry enough. Her mother had capitulated and bought another bottle, leaving it on Susan's dresser without another word. Susan would have to use it more sparingly, but Alexis was one of her best customers, so she could have a splash this time.

The bottle did its job and perked Alexis back up. Susan got to work. She was always envious of Alexis' skin. It was porcelain-perfect. When she did get zits, they even managed to be cute, not bulbous and oozing like Susan's. Alexis' mom let her get chunky highlights that were only a little bit grown out, and Susan envied that, too.

Makeup was one thing, but chemicals on her head was a step too far in her mother's opinion. A last little flick of purple on the outer corners of the lid to bring out the green in Alexis' eyes, and Susan stepped back, pleased. Just as Susan reached for the Precious Plum, another student called out as they passed by. Susan looked up to wave. When she looked back down, the lipstick was nowhere to be found. Dropping to her knees, Susan searched under the desk and came back up empty handed. As she was standing back up, Susan the passenger spotted the back edge of the black tube poking out from just underneath the lockers.

Alexis had never stolen it. Susan hadn't spotted it back then. Oh, no. Susan expected to feel a little sick, but she didn't. Well, not anymore sick then she normally felt on meal-skip days. And she was about to falsely accuse her friend and best customer of stealing lipstick that she had simply lost.

"Aardvark." The tingles returned, and Susan squeezed her eyes shut expecting the tiny points of pain, but they never came. Cautiously, she opened one eye. Then the other. Her middle school was gone, as was Alexis. Aurora stood in front of the same door Susan had stepped through moments ago.

"You didn't want to finish the memory?"

Susan shook her head. "No. No, I remember what happened."

"What happened?"

"I accused her of stealing. She said she didn't. I insisted. We both cried. I was so angry and couldn't understand why she was angry. She didn't get to be angry. She stole from me."

"But she didn't steal from you. And you didn't believe her."

"Well, I know that now." Susan barked. She needed to move. She always needed to move when she felt cornered.

Susan walked seven steps up the green carpet, pivoted, and returned. Aurora did not try to follow her. She remained in front of the door, unmoving except for her head, which turned to follow Susan's pacing. "We stopped speaking to each other that day. Her family moved away the next year, but still, I ended that friendship over nothing."

"I know." There was no judgment in Aurora's voice. But Susan felt like there should have been.

"Over nothing. Over an accident. I probably knocked that lipstick off the desk myself. I didn't just stop being her friend. I…" Susan cut herself off, speeding up her pace and adding two more steps to her path.

"What did you do?" Aurora asked, her voice still so tolerant, it was a little abrasive.

"I may have started a few rumors about her."

"May have?" Aurora clarified.

"Fine. Yes. I told everyone that Alexis Johnson gave blowjobs behind the band house. I don't think anyone believed me, though."

"They did." Aurora said.

"They did what?"

"Believe you." Susan let her eyes close, her shoulders deflating.

"Oh. Well. Did she know it was me?

"She did." The guide confirmed.

"Well, that makes me feel like a pile of shit."

"Why?"

"Why does knowing that Alexis knew I outright lied about her make me feel like a pile of shit? Is that what you need clarification on?" Susan felt the broiler turn on just under her breastbone, the familiar flash of heat that she normally used to fuel her most severe tongue lashings.

"No. Why didn't you feel like a piece of shit for lying about her in the first place?" Aurora asked, her voice still calm and irritatingly neutral.

"Excuse me?" The heat in Susan's chest roared to an engulfing flame of rage.

"You didn't say you felt like a piece of shit until you learned Alexis knew you'd spread those rumors. You only felt bad once you knew you'd been caught."

"That's not true."

"Is it not?"

"No! It's not true!" Susan bit out. "Just because I didn't say it doesn't mean I didn't feel it." She'd stopped her pacing, and every cell would have been vibrating if she'd still been made of cells. Since she was apparently just a ball of

Susan-shaped energy, she wasn't vibrating. She was just hanging there in space.

"Very good, then." Aurora demurred. "Were there any other memories you wanted to revisit?"

"Decidedly not." Susan decreed. "That little experiment in self-punishment was enough, I think. Let's move this along. You said I get to choose the next life, so what are my options? Is there a catalogue or something?"

"I understand your request. This next part is about really drilling down into what your soul is taking away from being Susan Chambers. This is the part of the After Death that is both wonderfully comforting and uncomfortably wonderful. We have a few memories I'd like to make sure you revisit. Our data suggests you need to confront a few things for the good of your soul's experience, via the life you just completed." Aurora's teeth flashed as she spoke.

"I thought I got to choose the memories to relive." Susan challenged.

"You do. And if in between these moments of exploration you think of some other memory you'd like to revisit, just let me know. Same with the questions. You're in control here."

"Then I'd rather not confront anything."

"I understand, and we can take as long as you'd like to get through this next part. But while you're in control, I do have a job to do as your guide. And that means that I will have to make you confront a few things about Susan Chambers."

"Feels like a bait and switch, to me."

Aurora lifted her hand and tucked a slice of her bobbed hair behind her ear. It made her look more childlike. "I can see how you'd view it that way, yes."

"Then you acknowledge you changed the rules?"

"I didn't change anything. I called myself a guide for a reason. There are a few things I must guide you to and through. If you incorrectly assumed what the rules are and are not, I can't help that supposition. I can only work to correct it moving forward."

"You're annoying."

"Many would say the same about you." Aurora spoke as if it was simply a statement of fact. Susan was jarred at this woman's audacity. She felt her chin retract, her head rocking back on her neck.

"Rude."

"Many would say that about you too."

Susan's tolerance for this woman hit rock bottom. "What's with the tone shift? You were nice a second ago. Holy shit. Feeling a little attacked."

"I'm still being nice. This is the hall of memories. If you're feeling attacked, I'm not the one launching the assault." Aurora's chin dipped, and she peered at Susan through her lashes.

Susan chewed on her tongue, letting her jaw slide from one side to the other before nodding, her lips pursed. "Okay, I'll bite," Susan wasn't sure she truly wanted to know this, but she asked anyway. "Many people would call me annoying and rude. But how would most people describe me? Like the majority of people who ever met me… what would they say?" Aurora made a face Susan couldn't read, and her gaze drifted upward again. When her eyes snapped back to Susan's, Aurora spoke in a crisp, even tone.

"Susan Chambers was an annoying, rude, bossy bitch." Susan thought she might have preferred to face off with the bus again for as hard as that sentence slammed into her chest. But Aurora wasn't done. "She was a work-a-holic with a selfish and vindictive streak. She put her needs above all others. She held grudges like it was a second job and had absolutely no qualms speaking her mind, regardless of context or the feelings of those who heard her."

Aurora spoke as casually as someone reading the menu at a vegan pop-up restaurant. "However, most would also report that she was not stingy and would apply all available resources to solve a problem. She was driven, incredibly creative, one of the top experts in her field, an award-winning marketer who was uniquely focused and quite motivating." Susan was about to argue more, but that last word caught her by surprise.

"I was motivational?" Susan had often dreamed of being a motivational speaker. Her most replayed bathroom mirror fantasy was giving her TedTalk with a Dyson blower-brush as a microphone and slide show pictures drawn in the fogged glass of the shower door. Aurora pulled yet another unreadable face.

"You were motivating. That's different than motivational."

"How so?" Susan felt like the air was thinner than it should have been. Was there even air here?

"People wanted to do their best around you and for you to avoid your ire. They weren't performing their best to earn your praise. They were doing it so you wouldn't yell at them."

A flurry of emotions slammed into Susan so hard, it almost made her lose balance. Guilt, anger, shame, more anger. She raised a pointer finger to really get going with the waggling in this snide little brat's face, and then she stopped. Aurora didn't even flinch. She just watched, her unremarkable hazel eyes alight. 'Susan Chambers was an annoying, rude, bossy bitch' looped in Susan's head. Selfish? Vindictive? She stood watching the upraised digit for what could have been minutes or months. She didn't know. Ceding the staring contest with her own appendage, Susan let her hand drop as she looked at Aurora.

"You're saying I was a bad person."

"No. That might be what you heard. But that's not what I said."

"But the way you described me. You're not wrong. I was annoying and rude and overbearing… I mean, look what I was capable of when I was twelve. Over a damn lipstick. And I didn't outgrow that. Holy shit." Susan didn't remember starting to pace again, but when she looked up, she was at least ten feet from where Aurora still waited by the door, watching and listening.

"I was, generally and specifically, a bitch. Oh. Fuck." Susan's knees wobbled and threatened to fail. She spun around looking for a chair or a bench in the hall that she knew full well was barren, save the carpet and the sconces, but she desperately wanted a sit. Aurora reached her with surprising speed, reaching behind Susan to open a door that had not been there a moment ago.

As the door swung open, more of that nostalgia flooded Susan's not-real veins. An entire living room sprawled out before her, complete with a rattan couch flanked by matching chairs. A peach stucco entertainment center surrounded a giant cabinet-style flat-screen TV in the center of the wall opposite the couch. Aurora strode to the sofa and lowered herself gingerly, her ankles tucking back so her silhouette formed a wonky Z shape. The guide stretched out a hand and patted the couch cushion beside her.

Susan let her feet stumble forward. More of a fall than a walk, she let her knees buckle as she spun and plopped. Staring at shadowy silhouette in the darkened screen, she mentally scolded herself for the plopping. It was neither dignified nor graceful. Her mother would have had a conniption at it.

"We either embrace our femininity or we say 'fuck it' and move to a hippie compound. And I don't know about you, but I like soap." Susan had heard that, or something similar, a thousand times through her childhood and a million more times in her own head, always in her mother's voice. Anytime Susan was considering being distinctly unladylike, she heard the refrain. It hadn't always stopped her from being unladylike, but she heard it all the same.

Aurora spoke softly. "What is a bad person?" She sounded like a therapist, each letter of each word definitive and intentional.

Susan was stunned by the question. Or perhaps she was just in shock at the realization that she was a bad person—or at least a highly dislikable one. She couldn't be surprised. Susan knew who she was. But to sit with it still hurt.

"I don't know. Someone who is ugly inside no matter what they show out?"

"That's platitudinal. It's a lot of words that say nothing. Say something this time. What is a bad person?" Aurora asked again, sounding more like a marketer than a therapist now. Susan would know; she'd talked to hundreds of both.

"Someone who does bad things." Susan knew she sounded like a child, but Aurora nodded. Therapist-y.

"And what is a bad thing?" Aurora implored. Susan didn't want to follow her down this path. She threw her hands out, exasperated. *Ladies don't wildly gesticulate,* her mother's voice crowed.

"I don't know. Bad things are bad." Aurora's brow dropped over her eyes as she peered at Susan. "I don't know, Aurora," Susan challenged. Her skin was crawling with the confrontation and she hated it. She felt slimy.

"We'll try again. A bad person does bad things. What bad things do bad people do?" came Aurora's pressing demand, this time back to the marketer voice. Susan took a deep breath, and then another, before she replied.

"They hurt. They kill. They steal. They push over old blind ladies. They take good things and ruin them."

"And is that what you did? Did you take good things and ruin them?" Aurora pushed, her tone still too goddamn pleasant.

"No!" said Susan, defensiveness coating the word. "I mean, I'd like to think I took okay things and improved them. I took good things and made them better. At least, that's what I was trying to do." She despised the whine she couldn't strip out of her tone.

"Then by your own definition, you were not a bad person." Aurora said nonchalantly. Susan opened her mouth to argue but stopped short.

"But the way I treated people could have been kinder. You said I was motivating, not motivational."

"You might have had some rather forward ways of communicating, but you weren't exactly pushing over old blind ladies."

"No. But I hurt people. Maybe not by clubbing them over the head. But I wielded my words like a weapon. And I was proud of my ability to do that. I was proud of nailing people to a wall with my vocabulary. I used my voice to manipulate people into doing what I wanted." The words were spilling out of her, and she was about to continue when she realized exactly where she was sitting, and then the words drained away. The rattan sofa, the disconcertingly orange stucco: she'd been here before. It was her childhood best friend's living room.

Susan's best friend growing up had been Mary Stinson, by way of their mothers being best friends. Born just a month apart, Susan and Mary had grown up permanent fixtures in each other's orbits through their early childhoods. Mary

Lou and her mother, Evelyn, lived next door to Susan and her mother, Elizabeth.

The Stinson house was a paramount of eighties, young-urban-professional decor that Mary Lou's mother steadfastly clung to well into the nineties. Everything in that house was a shade of peach, coral, mint, or brown. Things that had no business being stone were made to look like stone using gobs of plaster. Disembodied heads with stretched and twisted mouths stood on stands next to limbless mannequin forms with paint splattered across them. Sculptures of glass stretched curling fingers out toward bowls filled with shiny balls, sea stars, starfish, and shells.

The furniture might have been the height of '80s interior design, but at the time of Susan's memory, it felt more like lawn furniture that had been brought inside for the winter and never moved back out. The chairs were circular and the couch was oval, each with great sheets of rattan wrapping the back, a heavy arc of blonde wood forming the top of the back rests. The cushions were wrapped in thick upholstery fabric that featured blurry blobs of the coral, mint, and peach color scheme.

Overall, the furniture committed two crimes: It was ugly and uncomfortable. So poorly designed that when you leaned back, that beam hit right at your shoulder blades, and the cushions were entirely too thin to make any sort of difference. Susan had spent more time in this living room with the uncomfortable and ugly seating than she had her own living room, opulently appointed with baroque revival furniture.

"Why are we here?" Susan asked, taking in the exact replica of Mary's living room, each item meticulously chosen by Evelyn.

"This was a place you felt safest. I figured, for this part of the process, you'd feel more comfortable here."

"This is part of the process?" Susan said.

"Part of the process of preparing your soul for a new experience is breaking down the previous one to its sum parts. It's a reckoning, if you will. A chance to take in everything you learned throughout this span of existence. You don't retain the memories of your past lives, and when we leave this building, every experience this version of Susan Chambers ever enjoyed will remain here. You won't feel like Susan Chambers anymore, because you won't really be Susan Chambers, not exclusively. But the experience and wisdom will remain. Those lessons, those nuggets of ethereal compassion, or hardening, shape your soul. Some lives a soul lives teaches them a great deal. Others offer very little."

"A life wasted, then?" Susan felt morose despite the forcibly chipper room.

"A little is not necessarily a waste."

"How else would you view a life that offered nothing of value to a soul that lives quadrillions of years over, what? Billions or trillions of life spans?"

"Well, you're assuming a life can only offer value through deeds and doings. Great humans throughout history lived the most valuable lives. But your own soul has lived unfairly short lives, in which absolutely nothing was accomplished, but that were tremendously valuable."

"I don't understand what you mean by that. Nothing was accomplished, but it was valuable?"

"No existence is worthless. The life your soul experienced immediately prior to being born as Susan Chambers lasted precisely fifty-seven minutes and still offered some important lessons in the fragility of life and the positive impact of fear," Aurora explained.

"Oh, my god. That's horrible," Susan felt in her hand an urge to drift up to clutch her invisible pearls, but she bade it remain in her lap. She flexed it to soothe the impulse. "But also, it sounds a little derivative. Perhaps that baby's parents could learn some things from a life that short, but it's unlikely anything useful or instructive happened in less than an hour."

"Oh, you weren't a baby. At least not a human infant. And your parents in that life didn't even know you'd been born. You were an ant. You had just hatched in the nursery of a rather large ant colony in rural Nebraska. The farmer who owned the land poured molten aluminum into the ant hill, killing most of the colony, some ten thousand souls gone for the sake of art, including the ant housing your soul."

Susan shuddered at that. "I've seen those sculptures. They are beautiful, but they always gave me the heebie-jeebies." Another shudder rippled across her shoulder blades. "They were so creepy and unnerving. Good god, that sounds like a horrific way to die. Drowning in molten…" Susan's hand covered her mouth, and she found she couldn't finish verbalizing the thought. "That was a phobia of mine. A strangely specific phob…" The word trailed to nothingness as the realization settled.

"Wow. That was quick." Aurora quipped.

"That part of the woo-woo is true." Susan gasped in quiet disbelief. One of her girlfriends, Kayley, had forever been hopping from one spiritual identity to another. During one of her ethereal periods, she hosted a seance to commune with the spirits on the other side of the veil. Susan had agreed on a whim to attend. Kayley had confidently pronounced that one's biggest fear or phobia was the way they died in their previous life. Susan had scoffed, not believing in reincarnation or cycling at all, but that patchouli-scented, sage-smudging bitch had been right.

"'That part of the woo-woo,' as you call it, is true." Aurora echoed. "That's another one of those leaks that we aren't able to explain. But the next life your soul experiences will be deathly afraid of busses, bike racks, or brain damage. Potentially all three, depending on what sort of life you choose to experience."

"Good to know. Maybe I should choose something that doesn't have to deal with those. One of those Jell-O flashlight beings, perhaps? Although I guess everything has a brain. No matter what I choose, I'll be afraid of brain damage I suppose."

"Actually, no. That species does not have a brain. Kind of like jelly fish. It's more like a neural network. So, if you choose Jell-O flashlight, you would not have to fear brain damage. Just busses and bike racks there."

"They have no brains, but they have busses and bike racks?" Susan asked.

"Yes."

"If they have bike racks, they must have bikes. Does the species of congealed light have legs?"

"Most of the time." Aurora was so nonchalant about this, that Susan let it drop. "Do you still feel you were a bad person?" Aurora recentered the conversation that had derailed so fantastically. Susan appreciated that master move.

"Does it matter if I was a good person or a bad person if the memories are gone once I move on to the next life?"

"You tell me."

"I mean, this soul managed to glean something out of being an ant for fifty-some-odd minutes," Susan said. "There had to be something useful in forty-two years."

"I'm sure there was. What was it?"

"What was what?"

"What was the something useful in forty-two years?"

"I don't know, but I'm sure my soul or this soul, however you're supposed to say it…" Susan waved her hand dismissively and Aurora corrected her.

"It's your soul."

"Okay, my soul. But I'm sure it's got the lessons already packed away. Whether or not I feel I was a good person is irrelevant."

"I understand how you drew that conclusion, but it is partially wrong." Aurora's head drifted to the side as she considered how to proceed. "Whether or not you feel you were a good person is the most relevant thing here. Potentially, the *only* relevant thing here. The ability to decide and embrace whether you were a good person or a bad person might be that nugget your soul takes away from its time being Susan Chambers."

"And when we finish here, I will cease to exist." Susan said. She flexed her hand in her lap once more. Part of her disliked this idea that she just would no longer be, but part of her sort of understood this was always going to be the way. Susan Chambers had never really subscribed to a religion. They all felt like little more than glorifying old men dangling sky cake in front of their followers. This old guy said his sky cake was better than that old crone's. And this group of eternally young brigands swore their sky cake topped all the other ones. But it was just promises and teasing of imaginary shit. Though it wasn't as comforting as she'd expected, she did feel a modicum of solace in that at least she was right about the sky cake thing. No sky cake. Just a big house full of nostalgia and then a blink into nothingness.

Aurora took a deep breath, or at least appeared to, and then began again. "Your soul is you, and you are your soul. Someday, yes, it may cease to exist, but likely not for an incredibly long time. Longer than you or I can grasp, realistically. A quadrillion years is almost an unfathomable amount of time. A trillion, a billion… All of those feel more like silly words rather than measurements of volume or time. And we struggle to understand just how much that is. For now, everything that makes you Susan Chambers will carry on."

"But I won't remember being Susan Chambers." Susan protested.

"But you'll still have been Susan Chambers. You don't remember being born, but not remembering the process doesn't change that you did experience being born.

Technically speaking, depending on how and who you become in your next life, you could encounter Susan Chambers, or at least the evidence of her existence. You won't necessarily know to do that. But everything Susan Chambers was has left a mark on the souls around her. She existed, *you* existed, for better or worse."

Susan felt herself spiraling. "Yeah, it's that 'for worse' part that has me all up in my feels, as the kids would say." Susan had never gotten around to having kids, and by the time she realized it, her ovaries had packed up shop and started to turn in for the perimenopausal winter. But her older brother, Samuel, had himself a whole brood, including the old soul Mikayla, and Susan had prided herself on spoiling those children rotten.

She had plenty of money, few extravagant interests, save her shoe collection, a pod wardrobe with high-quality pieces that swapped out every few years, annual trips to Italy, and an insistence that she fly first class everywhere. She had the resources to buy the children in her life all their little hearts desired.

Just a few weeks ago, she and her brother had argued about Susan buying Cavanaugh, Samuel's youngest, a pony. "We live in Hyde Park, Susan. Where the hell are we going to put a pony? I don't know that the building will take kindly to converting our parking spot to a stable." Samuel had an excellent point there, but it was Susan's nature to argue. Especially with him.

"Pay the right amount to the right person, and pretty much any rule is negotiable," had been Susan's counter. Susan now realized that Samuel was sure to win the pony debate by way of Susan taking a bus to the brain stem.

Samuel and Susan had never been close growing up. Their father had been a pharmacy salesman for some drug company and was always on the road, so the care and raising of the children was left squarely on their mother's shoulders. She handled Samuel by packing his schedule to the brim with a thousand and one sports and extracurriculars. Susan remembered her mother often lamenting that she didn't know what she was supposed to do with a boy; weren't they their father's problem? Samuel was easier to deal with if he always had something to do and someplace to be.

It was Susan who earned all their mother's direct attention.

"Girls are trained to be women by their mothers."

"A young girl should not be left to fend for herself."

Those had been regular lectures and quippy catchphrases her mother wielded like weapons. Susan was never left to flounder or figure things out on her own. Her mother had been glued to her side every step of her childhood. From piano lessons to a brief stint in princess pageants to Susan's dreadful single season in dance, Susan and her mother worked as one. However, that uneven attention resulted in Samuel and Susan often being pitted against each other as children.

Samuel would get slapped with "why can't you be more like your sister?" whereas Susan ended up with "boys like your brother don't turn out to be men worth much of anything at all." Even once both siblings realized their primary guardian might have missed the mark on some of that thinking, the rift between them had grown almost too wide to bridge. Susan often wondered if her attempt to spoil Samuel's children was some half-assed way of trying to stay connected to her brother. Aurora's voice sliced through the reverie.

"It's upsetting to you that you feel you might have been a bad person?" Aurora asked calmly.

"Well, of course it's upsetting." The words rocketed out of Susan. "No one wants to get to the end of their life and realize they sucked ass the whole time and everyone hated them. Didn't Dickens write a whole fucking cautionary tale about this?" Susan hadn't meant to yell, but she had. Aurora was unphased.

"You've decided you were a bad person as Susan Chambers, then?"

"At the very least, I was a heartless bitch."

"Oh?"

"What do you mean, 'oh'? Like you're surprised. You know as much about me as I know, apparently."

"I am surprised. And I do know as much about you as you do. Arguably more, as I have access to memories you've forgotten. And were it my call to make—and it's not, it's wholly yours—I don't know that I'd label you a heartless bitch."

"What would you label me?"

"Irrevocably focused."

"Now who's being platitudinal?"

"That's fair." Aurora chuckled. "I guess I'd say you were fixated on a series of goals, and those around you either helped you accomplish those goals or hindered your progress. Those you felt hindered you, you sought to either move the obstacle they created or carve a new path around them. For those who supported you, you were incredibly giving. Maybe not in a traditional shirt-off-your-back sort of way, but you paid off an assistant's student loans once."

"Yeah. And then I fired her."

"But why did you fire her? You gave her a very specific reason."

Susan began to answer, but then realized she didn't quite remember why she fired that woman. She remembered her being sweet, and Susan didn't always take to sweet people. "I... I don't remember."

"You could... just ask." Aurora replied, a slow smile warming her eyes.

Susan engaged in the briefest moment of internal warfare. When curiosity won, she said, "Let me see that memory, please."

"Ooh. A please. Do bad people say 'please'?" Aurora said, raising one eyebrow and pursing her lips playfully. Without further explanation, Aurora pointed to the door behind Susan, the same one she'd entered her childhood best friend's living room through. Susan rose, crossed the room in three strides, and yanked open the door.

Stepping through, she stood before a beautiful woman with an umber complexion and night-dark hair coiling out of her head in a diaphanous cloud. She'd teased it out so it became somewhat sheer toward the edges, darkening and solidifying as it came closer to her face. Sometimes it was tamped down into the shape of a heart or a puffy little cloud. Some days a star, or twisting and coiling through itself in intricate serpentine plaits. Today, it was a simple but elegant puffball with dots of twinkling gems strategically placed throughout.

Christine Caldwell had always done the absolute most with her outfits, given that she was working with next to nothing. Today she was wearing a silk scarf, tied in a specific way to form two diamonds that covered her generous breasts, held in place with a belt, some incredibly trustworthy knots, and a sparkling dragonfly pin secured in that space between those assets on display. Paired with a hip-highlighting flouncy skirt and a fetching blazer, Susan suspected she could have been in a magazine feature or on a runway.

Susan knew for a fact that those red bottoms were achieved with OPI Nail Polish, rather than Christian Louboutin. If image was everything, Christine was well on her way to having it all.

As the marketing director for a fashion house, having an assistant that might also have been a model wasn't unusual. Nor was it taboo to have boob scarves masquerading as blouses. Susan didn't have the figure to pull it off, but her assistant did.

"Christine, for fuck's sake, how did you triple book me? It's a calendar. There's a visual representation of what is available and what is not. If there's a big green block on the calendar, don't add anything else." Christine said nothing in response, keeping her head down and eyes trained on her dollar-store designer shoes. "This is not the first time this has happened. But it will be the goddamn last. You're fired, Ms. Caldwell."

Christine's head snapped up. "No, please. Ms. Chambers, please you can't fire me."

Susan was repulsed by the instant decay into begging. "It took me nine months to find this job, and I need it. I need to be here. I promise, I'll do better. I will personally explain to all three of the attendees that I'm the idiot. And

I will do better. Please. Please don't fire me!" Christine clasped her hands together in supplication.

"Oh, my dear Christine. Find your damn dignity. Pleading is unladylike," Susan spat. Christine looked abashed. "What did you get a degree in, anyway, because it certainly couldn't be business? Not if Outlook bests you."

"Oh. Um." Christine fumbled over her words for a moment, and it made Susan want to throw something. After several false starts that had Susan's eye twitching, the woman dribbled out, "F…Fashion Design. I…uh…I went to NYU, like you, and then Parsons." Susan let her eyes trail up and down Christine's get up with fresh perspective.

"Yes. I can see. Okay, then, you know what to do next. Go be a fashion designer and stop wasting anyone's time as a cut-rate, useless assistant."

"Ms. Chambers, I really wish I could, but start-up fashion lines don't exactly pay the bills. I can't design clothes and eat right now, much less pay rent and keep my student loans from eating me alive. I have to work my way up, and if you fire me, it'll be next to impossible to get my foot back in the door at any fashion house."

"Fine. I'll pay off your student loans and call it a 'downsizing.'" Christine gasped and took a step back. A look of sheer confusion blanketed her. "You're a waste of space as a secretary, but there might be an iota of potential somewhere underneath all that hair as a designer. And if student loans are the thing that keeps you beholden to doing work you're too incompetent to do, fine. Throwing cash at your creditors is doing a service to everyone you might otherwise fail. Go design something and get out of my office." Christine's mouth hung open, her arms slack at her side. "Go on, or I'll change my mind and black ball you instead. Get the fuck out."

"Aardvark." Susan said flatly.

"You seem less than enthused by this memory, Susan." Aurora said from behind her.

Susan blinked, and the glass-encased basket that had been her office at that fashion house was once again Mary Stinson's 1987-inspired living room. No tingles this time. "It's six of one, half a dozen of another. I didn't pay her loans off out of the kindness of my heart. I was cruel. I didn't need to be."

"Your cruelty shifted the course of her entire life." Aurora responded. "Because you paid her student loans, Christine Caldwell was able to do exactly what you told her to do. She enjoyed a very successful career as a fashion designer and even debuted a nominally successful line at New York fashion week with a collection titled, Chambered." Susan's eyebrow shot skyward. Aurora had the gall to look satisfied. "Very avant-garde stuff that translated to wearable garments. She never transcended to Versace or Chanel levels of notoriety, but she did find success and fulfillment."

"Hmm," was all Susan offered in response. She'd been staring at a basket full of wood chips and flower petals. For a moment, she remembered what those rose-scented wood chips tasted like. The nineties were plagued by a lot of things, but perhaps one of the greatest sins in Susan's estimation was the entire decade's obsession with both decorative soaps and potpourri. Her mother, Mary Lou's mother, every parent of every peer was plagued by scented wood curls, nautical-themed soaps, and bowls of smelly stuff that served no other purpose than to occupy space once the thin layer of aromatic oil evaporated. Susan had eaten plenty of potpourri thinking it was candy, never learning from her past mistakes on that front.

"That's not a sound one makes when one is convinced," Aurora quipped.

Susan broke eye contact with the bowl of not-candy. "I'm in marketing. I understand how case studies and stat lines can be manipulated to tell the story you need the client to hear. One success story does not necessarily solidify my greatness."

"Is greatness your goal here?"

"Isn't greatness always the goal?" Susan was feeling snippy.

"No. Not by a long shot," Aurora responded simply. "Plenty of people are satisfied with mediocrity, good enough, and as good as it's going to get."

"Well, I never was, so to relive this is a bit of a depressing little lark."

"You feel that paying off a person's student loans, thereby opening up a path to success and fulfillment, isn't a step toward greatness?"

"It's not that I'm trying to show false humility here. It's great that my being a bitch meant that someone else got their dream job. It's that I remember—vividly, thanks to the instant replay—how I felt: I legitimately wanted her away from me. She was pathetic as an assistant. I spent more time fixing her work than doing mine for those what, six? Seven? months she was in my employ. I paid those loans because I didn't want to deal with her at all. Not in references. Not in HR. I just wanted her gone and dealt with, and that was the first and easiest way that occurred to me. I wasn't helping her. I was… how did you put it? Moving an obstacle."

"I'd wager Christine Caldwell would say differently."

"Like I said, six of one, half a dozen of another." Susan swished her hand through the air as if trying to the clear the air of a foul stench.

"You still think you were a bad person?" Aurora sounded more like she was musing aloud rather than asking Susan a direct question.

"I think a broken clock is right twice a day. I helped Christine Caldwell clear the pathway to her potential, and she was clever enough to seize that chance. But I also know without having to replay that I tanked several careers, made miserable hundreds of others, and outright destroyed several lives using their hands, backs, necks, and heads as stepping stones. I'm sure my soul will be quite relieved to choose another life and potentially not be such a raging thundercunt this time around."

"You are your soul. It's the same thing. In this moment and place in time and space, your soul and Susan Chambers are the same. Let me ask you a different question along the same vein here," Aurora said. "Is it a bad thing to have been a bad person?"

"What kind of question is that?" Susan asked incredulously.

"It's a question meant to be considered in order to trigger deeper exploration. Is it a bad thing to have been a bad person?"

"I mean, yes. It's bad to be bad. These are preschool concepts, here. We don't want to be bad."

"Why don't we want to be bad? That's a little bigger than a preschool concept overall."

Susan started to give an answer, but the words caught in her throat. She'd always excelled at thinking on her feet. She was a nimble thinker, and the ability to spin a great explanation or a heart-rending plea in milliseconds had gotten Susan out of several scrapes, including groundings, tickets, bad deals, and catching the blame for a few nominal mistakes that might have been career-enders, had she not talked her way out of them with a quickness.

"We don't want to be bad…" Susan started and still had no idea where to go with that sentence. She tried again. "We don't want to be bad…" It was at this point that she might have felt a flush crawl up her neck if she'd had a neck. Lacking that, she only felt annoyed and slightly embarrassed. More emphatically this time, she spat out, "We don't want to be bad because that's how society works. We must be nominally empathetic in how we interact with each other at the very least, and compassionate and deeply understanding ideally, or we end up as chaotic, half-brained Neanderthals clubbing each other for a hunk of half-rotted cow." The words had spilled out of her, but aside from the rather tortured caveman analogy, she was pleased. And a little surprised with herself. Her hands pulled together, her thumb rubbing a circle across one palm.

"And what is bad, again? I'm not sure we took the time to look at what is bad and what is good. We defined what a bad person was, in a way, but not what makes something bad."

"I know you're going to have some weird look or snark at this but, honestly, and I mean I've considered this…"

As expected, that damn eyebrow of Aurora's was creeping toward her hairline again. Susan amended, "Or at least I've considered it just now but feel confident in what I'm about to say: Bad is anything that isn't good. Good is anything that isn't bad. I could use more words, but we're sort of in subjective territory here. What is bad to me or for me might not be bad to someone else. Occam's razor. The simplest explanation is often the most correct one. The simple balance of 'bad is not good' and 'good is not bad' holds up here."

For the second time in a matter of seconds, Susan was floored by her own words, her own thoughts. She'd never been one to wax philosophic unless she was trying to indulge one of those over-educated pedantic types who liked believing they had a unique thought in their head.

"Oh," was all Aurora said, but it sounded more impressed than inquisitive. "This is a new tune you're singing."

"How so?"

"You just admitted something that proves that maybe you're not the bad person you think you might be." Aurora paused as if waiting for Susan to interject, but Susan just watched, waiting for more. "You said that 'good' and 'bad' are subjective terms. And what is bad for you might not be bad for someone else."

"Well, yes, in general terms we can't really define what a bad thing is without a lot more context. The question of whether I was a bad person is subject to my discretion and the discretion of those I interacted with or impacted.”

“Would Christine Caldwell describe you as a bad person?”

The first thought that occurred to Susan in response to this was a stalwart ‘yes,’ but she paused before letting that affirmation escape. “She’d describe me as a bitch, certainly.”

“Don’t obfuscate. Answer.”

Susan’s head twitched to the side. Aurora could be pushy when she wanted to.

“I guess, no. She might not like me very much, but I don’t think she’d describe me as a bad person, especially given how my being a bitch ended up a positive for her.”

Aurora watched. Susan watched back, wondering at the wisdom of a staring contest with someone who knew or could find out literally anything about Susan Chambers with just a glance toward the ceiling. Aurora broke first to do just that, look at the ceiling.

“I’d now like to take you into another memory from your life.” Aurora stood from the rattan sofa, running her palms over the pencil skirt to smooth the gathers of fabric across her thighs. Her heels, a generic brand Susan couldn’t identify by sight, clicked across the tile floor. A few steps had taken her to the door which should have led to the kitchen. “I’d like to talk about your time at Coconut Express.”

"Why?" Susan felt defensive for a reason she couldn't identify. Coconut Express had been her first "big girl" marketing job. It had also been an unmitigated disaster at the end.

"Because I'm making a point."

"That's not nebulous or ominous at all."

"Good. It wasn't meant to be."

"You're steering this self-discovery now?" Susan asked.

"I've been steering it the whole time, Susan." Aurora replied—not haughtily, however. Susan thought she might need to be offended by her guide's tone but decided not to be. Aurora pushed open the swinging door and revealed the hallway once more.

The guide gestured with her head. Susan sighed heavily and scanned the room. The decor might have been criminal, but everything else about Susan's memories in that room was pleasant. More than pleasant. Susan had always felt more at home at Mary and Evelyn's than her own childhood house. When she fondly thought of family dinners, it was dinners eaten with Mary's family at the Stinson house.

"Did you want to revisit any memories from this place?" Aurora asked, though her eyes were focused upward once more. Her gaze rejoined Susan's. "Perhaps the sleepover when you were ten and watched your first horror movie?” Susan's expression was accidental as she recalled exactly how that had gone.

Mary Lou had wanted to watch *The Exorcist*, and Susan, not knowing any better, had agreed. A quick trip to Blockbuster on their bikes, a few trips around the kitchen to gather popcorn and movie snacks, and they settled in on the pointless cushions.

By the time the possessed girl's head was spinning around, Mary Lou was near tears. Susan was unimpressed. It wasn't scary; it was corny. The special effects didn't look special enough, while the characters spent a lot of time creating their own problems and taking themselves too seriously. Susan had noticed how worried her friend was getting about such a silly movie, though. To ease her discomfort, Susan had started rattling off all the ways the movie got stuff wrong.

“Mary Lou, this movie is awful. Like, total snoozefest. If her head spun around that, it would snap her neck. I don't think demon possession would keep her head up after all that. Demons don't have bones. She'd just be all floppy.” Susan had let her head tip and loll across her shoulders. The distraction had worked, and Mary Lou laughed out a bit of her tension. They continued absolutely destroying the remainder of the movie, laughing at all the parts that were supposed to be scary for how silly they looked.

Susan half chuckled, half huffed. "I think I just did, all on my own. Didn't even need your doors." Susan wasn't sure she wanted to see Mary Lou the same way she'd seen Alexis. It would have been too visceral.

Mary Lou had been her best friend until she suddenly wasn't. It hadn't been either girl's choice to stop being friends. Shortly after Susan and Mary Lou turned twelve, their mothers had a falling out. Susan had never known what that had been about, but when her mother got herself uninvited to the Stinson house, the feeling had been mutual, and the Stinson's were no longer welcome in the Chambers home, either. Both girls were caught in the feud.

Mary Lou attended a private school across town, while Susan attended the local public school. The girls had been forbidden to speak to each other after school and on the weekends. Susan had had no choice but to comply with her mother's demands here, and the friendship, neglected through forced absence, faded. Susan wasn't sure she could tolerate revisiting the friendship she'd done nothing to lose but lost anyway.

Susan kept silent as she stepped through the door, Aurora following close behind. Susan stepped aside to let Aurora lead the way, but the guide didn't move once the door clicked closed.

"Why is it a hallway if there's only one door?"

"There's not just one door. There are hundreds. Thousands. Tens of thousands. At least, there can be. I told you, it's a big building."

"I believe you. But we keep running circles through this one." Susan waved a hand at the door Aurora kept turning into a portal to Susan's past.

"It's a matter of what a soul needs to ease the transition from one life to the next. Technically, we don't need the doors at all. We can simply start playing a memory. But as a soul adjusts to being in the After Death, we start with very well-known patterns of behavior. For souls that have just finished a human life, we use a hall and doors. Because that somehow makes sense somewhere deep in your understanding of how things should work. A hall of memories with doors to your lived experiences tends to make it easier for a soul to navigate."

"But, again, you've only used the one door?"

"You didn't seem the kind to endure pointless meanderings down a hallway when I could just use the same door. And not every soul uses a hallway, necessarily, because it might not make sense with the reality that soul's previous existence experienced. If you'd just finished an existence as a raccoon, this would probably look more like a series of dens or, perhaps, alleys, depending on whether it was a country or a city raccoon."

"How do you guide a soul through the After Death that was recently a raccoon?" Susan remembered that her soul had previously been a non-human. "Or an ant, for that matter?"

"Well, I wouldn't. I don't speak raccoon or ant. But others in my department do." Aurora quipped.

"Raccoon and ant are languages?"

"Yes and no. They are means of communication, and while your understanding of language is a teeny bit over-simplified, we can apply that term well enough. Raccoon is a language just like ant, dog, emu, and lemur."

"Do you speak any…" Susan stabbed toward an appropriate adjective. "Animalian languages?" She was mostly sure "animalian" wasn't a word. Aurora opened her mouth and a series of clicks, hums, chirps, and whistles came out. It was loud. Surprisingly loud. Painfully loud. Though she knew it didn't actually hurt her ears, as she didn't have ears, Susan couldn't suppress the instinct to clap her hands over them. Aurora closed her mouth and the racket stopped. "What the fuck was that?!" Susan still screamed, though there was nothing to scream over.

"Dolphin." Aurora declared. "It's very loud because it's meant to travel through water," she explained before Susan managed to ask the question. "We can do away with the doors from here on out if you'd like," the guide offered.

"It is unnecessary at this point, I think."

"Very well." Aurora bobbed her head once. Susan blinked, and the sconce-lined hallway was replaced with an office that was trying entirely too hard to be hip.

Susan knew that office well. "Coconut Express." Susan muttered. Though she'd been standing, Susan found herself sitting in an orange chair that occupied one corner. Literally in the shape of the fruit, the cushions were designed to look like the pulp and membranes of an orange with a wedge cut out. Aurora was sitting in its matching kiwi partner. Coconut Express had been the trying-to-hard-to-be-witty company that had given Susan her start in marketing.

After graduation and completing a stint of internships, both paid and unpaid, Susan had landed a job as a content manager for one of those venture capital bro start-ups. It was the kind of company that was built from the ground up with the sole goal of being sold to some big tech corporation only to be dismantled again. Everything operated at a loss because the goal was to get Google or Facebook or Microsoft to buy it for millions. The tech bros would home in on a complaint from the masses or create a problem that never existed in the first place, get a whole bunch of users interested and hyping it, and position themselves as a thorn in the tech giants' pinky toe. Eventually, the mega-corps would cave, throw some money at the broskis, and fire everyone else on the project.

Which is exactly what happened to Susan, and she knew that was the goal. But she was pleased to have a job that didn't only involve fetching coffee, scheduling plane tickets, and picking up dry cleaning.

"Why are we here?"

"I want to talk about balance. In all things, your soul is seeking balance. Your soul is energy. Here, it is pure energy. No physical body and, technically speaking, no real rules binding it to what you understand as the laws of physics or biology."

"Wait, I'm not bound by laws of physics? Like if I wanted to, I could fly or bend spoons with my mind. *Matrix* 'I know kung-fu' type stuff?"

"Again, technically, yes. Just like you could be a cat, if you wanted to fly, you could, but you'd have to convince every bit of your soul that it's safe to do so. Given that in its last form you could not fly, and gravity was a bit of a risk to muck about with, that's a bigger task than you think. But you're welcome to try. When you're done, I'd still like to talk about Coconut Express."

"No. No need. I've been parasailing. It's probably similar."

"Spot on, actually." Aurora confirmed. "But balance. You are concerned you may have been a bad person, and you don't want to be bad. But what if that was the best thing you could have possibly been, if not for your sake, for everyone else's?"

Susan's eyes darted across the room as if looking for the rest of what Aurora was saying. Aurora pulled her lips into her mouth—a thinking face, if Susan had ever seen one. "A soul is the energy that gives motion to stillness, light to darkness, and life to the inanimate. But it also brings darkness to light and frenzy to quiet and fury to peace. It's balance. Bad people must exist. It is a universal constant. With no villains, there is no need for heroes."

"Yes, I know the schtick." Susan said impatiently, spinning her hand in a circle between the pair. "You can't appreciate the good without the bad, but it still feels like a shitty lot to draw to have to be the bad person just so some other soul gets to be a good person this round."

"Oh, it's not a lottery system. It is random, but that sort of thing, whether this life is a good or bad one, isn't pre-ordained or selected in advance. Good or bad, hero or villain, that's decided by the choices you make in the that existence."

"But why would anyone choose to be bad?" Susan realized she was whining and didn't quite care enough to stop.

"Did you choose to be bad?"

Susan's answering "No" was curt.

"Do you think anyone chooses to be bad?" Aurora was now wearing a sort of smug leer that Susan found irritating. Or perhaps that irritation stemmed from understanding Aurora's point this time before she had to break it down into itty-bitty tiny bits.

"No." Susan's reply fueled Aurora's smile. "No. I think most people we can confidently label as 'bad' really thought they were on the right side of history and everyone else was bat-shit crazy for not understanding where they were coming from."

"History is written by the victors. It's a matter of perspective versus intent."

"Balance." Susan simplified.

"Balance." Aurora agreed. "Do you want to tell me about what happened at Coconut Express, or shall we visit that memory in its entirety?"

"You're really going to make me sit through that shitshow?"

"I'm going to make you sit through a very precocious object lesson, yes." The office door zhuzhed open and Susan's first boss, named Preston, popped his head in.

"Susie-Q!" He trilled. "Suzy-bo-BOOZY! How was your weekend?" Preston stuck his hands out at ninety-degree angles to his hips and shimmied to her at her desk, where she was now sitting despite having been sitting with Aurora on the fruit furniture. Susan tried to turn her head but was unable to. She remembered she was in a memory. She had no control here, instead riding passenger to her own past.

"Always great! Because greatness is up to me!" Susan heard herself say in the weakest attempt at cheer and positivity. Susan had long tried to forget all those years she pretended she was one of those silver-lining, eternal optimists with a winning personality and emotional-support water bottles coated in sunshine stickers and motivational quotes. It had always been an act, but Susan had been a great actress.

She'd done four years of theater in high school but told no one after graduation. She loved the stage, but love doesn't pay bills or buy Jimmy Choo's. Eventually, the effort wore on her, rather than the performance. That strain had begun to show itself by this point in her career at Coconut Express.

"And you are grrreat!" To emphasize the offensively bad Tony the Tiger impression, Preston stabbed the air with his forefinger and then froze in the pose. Susan faked a laugh. Preston dropped his arm and fake laughed back. "Hey, we need you in the Hufflepuff Conference in ten, kay? Doesn't matter what you're doing or what deadline is dying. Hufflepuff. Ten."

"Got it, got it!" replied Susan. She felt a thick grin plaster itself onto the lower half of her face. This was 2010, and everyone her age was clinging to the worship of the boy who accidentally survived the world's dumbest snake-man. Add to that the start-up mentality of "make work fun and it's fun to work," and every modern-to-the-point-of-blandness office in the country had offices named after their pre-teen hyper fixations. Coconut Express was big into teenage wizards and Susan didn't care for it, but she couldn't afford to be picky.

Ten minutes later and she sat down into a dangerously overstuffed armchair, folding her legs underneath her, crisscross applesauce, balancing her thick laptop on a knee. All the rest of her "teammates," not just marketing but most everyone employed by Coconut Express, filed in, plopping down on giant black and yellow bean bags or wobble chairs shaped like balls with wings. A couple just sprawled out, propping their chins on their hands like school children, on the area rug shaped like a crest with either a beaver or a wombat sprawled across the center. Susan almost screamed "aardvark" at the oddness of mil-lennial work culture. Then the entire ownership "team" of the company filed in, designer coffees in hand.

"Well, I'm not gonna waste everyone's time. We all know about the buy-out option ongoing with Microsoft, and, frankly, everything was going great until it wasn't. We've been strong-armed here just a little, but despite our best efforts, the big-picture guys just won't agree to keep the staff. If we keep the staff, we forgo the buyout. If we forgo the buyout our credit line expires, and Microsoft buys up the debt and the stock and *boom:* hostile takeover territory. Bing Bong Bang. Microsoft owns the company and dumps the staff. The only thing Microsoft wants is the code. They will do anything to get the code."

"Except keep the backbone of the company," called out a blonde man wearing flip flops to Susan's left.

"Exactly. They see everything so clearly through their Window on the world." Preston looked disgustingly pleased with himself for that little pun extraordinaire. "Except the fact that code is built by people, and if you lose the people, what's the code really worth?" refrained Preston, one hand on his chest. Quiet murmurs of agreement and adulation rippled across the room.

"Stop with the bullshit, Preston." Susan called into the ambience of the kumbaya moment unfolding in Hufflepuff Conference. Every head swiveled and settled on her, mouths agape and eyes wide. "That's just a load of drivel and rot, and you know it."

Preston looked like a fish on land, mouth opening and closing. Susan didn't care. She continued, unspooling all the angst from under the oppressive weight of toxic positivity.

"You have not once viewed this company as a collection of people. We have been assets, no different than this stupid ass chair or the fucking printer. Expendable, disposable, and bargaining chips when convenient."

Preston's business partner, Alec, an exact replica of every-thing that made up Preston but of Indian descent, looked like he meant to protest, but Susan held up a single fin-ger. "Don't you speak. I am not done." Alec looked like he'd been reprimanded by a school nun. He dipped his head and averted his gaze. "You both took a little pile of mummy and daddy's money and made up some bullshit facade, so you felt like you were somehow contributing to society. This place doesn't do anything except give you pedantic dick faces somewhere to chase ass and feel like really, real big kids. Look at you with your fancy offices and comically large desks." She flung her arms wide, her peripheral vision catching one of her co-workers flinching at the suddenness of the move. "You didn't build fuck all. You didn't sell fuck all. We did." Susan gestured grandly at the assembled team of Coconut Express, draped chaoti-cally over fandom décor. "And it's not even very good."

The room's energy had changed now. When Preston had started speaking, Alec nodding emphatically beside him, they controlled the room. They directed the tone. Susan had just wrested that away from them and she was thrilled at how easy it was. It felt impossibly nice.

"Neither of you, nor any of your other circle-jerk wank-ers with degrees Daddy paid for, have touched a single line of code. Nor do you even know what the fuck it does. Go ahead, Preston. Enlighten us. What do we do here at Coconut Express?"

"I know what my company does. We are the bridge between the end user experience…"

"Stop. In plain, regular-person English. What. The fuck. Do we do here, Preston?" Susan felt a little pride swell at standing up to the prick.

"We…" Preston's eyes flicked back and forth, desperately searching for his explanation that Susan knew full well he couldn't produce. She was calling his bluff, but, honestly, she didn't know the answer herself. Her job in marketing didn't require she understand what the product did, just that those with the money to buy it did. "We help… users?" Susan rolled her hand on her wrist, urging him to keep on keeping on. "Users connect with… um… wait, I know."

"No, you fucking don't." This was a new voice from the back of the room. An absolute mouse of a man that, until that moment, Susan had heard speak maybe twice. He was Korean and kept to himself and his delicious-smelling lunches. He was also one of the lead developers. If anyone in this room knew what exactly the precious Microsoft-coveted code of Coconut Express did, it was this little man. Park Hyun-ki. Probably. Susan couldn't quite remember. A flame of shame kindled low in her belly. She was in the memory, reliving it, and couldn't remember the man's name. Which means she hadn't really known it then. She didn't know why that made her feel bad, but it did.

"You don't know what the code you're selling does." There was a lilting accent to his words. His voice was soft but still powerful as he picked up steam. "I know you don't because, once, you walked into my office and asked to see what I was working on. I showed you, and you asked if I could, and I quote, 'translate all that Japanese' into a Word document for you to review. It was the Visual Studio, the development environment. You looked directly at the code and thought I was reading something in Japanese." Susan felt the edges of a grin tug the corners of her mouth upward. Preston just stood there. Park Hyunki exploded from his throne-shaped chair. "I AM NOT JAPANESE, YOU RACIST FUCK!"

"You thought he was Japanese?" A woman's voice said from her perch on an owl-shaped beanbag. That was the gal from Human Resources, with another unremembered or unknown name. A waterfall of red hair cascaded from her scalp to brush the edge of her chevron infinity scarf.

"We make a notification platform, Preston." This was one of Susan's teammates in marketing. "Rather than open a bunch of different websites to check on their connections and interactions and posts, Coconutters can see all their updates on one dashboard. Basically, we built a bunch of scrapers and pointed them at the most popular websites and services." The woman sounded disappointed. Then she gasped. "Holy shit." This came out of Susan's co-worker as a dark, sardonic giggle. "You don't know what we do. You don't have one goddamn clue." Murmurs of disgust and discontent swarmed the room like mildly annoyed bees.

"Is Microsoft actually buying the code? Or are you just selling the IP and cutting losses because you're bored?" This was Park Hyun-ki again. Susan stood down and let the room devour the boy in his alligator polo.

"Aardvark."

Aurora was before her once more, the gaudy conference room swapped out for the master bathroom of the house Susan and her ex-husband, Kevin had shared for the duration of their marriage. They'd cut corners at their wedding and kept it small, celebrating frugally. The newly minted couple used the money saved to buy a modest townhouse together. Located in Manhattan, but barely, it met their needs and fit the budget.

Susan knew most of her contemporaries valued a nice kitchen or a bit of green space for a dog to piss in. But for Susan, every dollar of value was holed up in a spa-level bathroom and a closet fit for a queen. A jetted, heated tub, a vanity that would have made half the socialites in New York green with envy, and the coup de grace, the steam room. The cedar lined room had been her refuge. Kevin hated the heat, and the steam fogged up his glasses, so he never went in there. If she wanted to escape him, the steam room was where she headed. She'd loved very little about that house, but that bathroom she'd have taken with her to the end of time.

Looking around it now, she supposed she had, in a way. It was the end of her time, and she was back in the bathroom she loved so much. Before she could overthink it, Susan moved, hand already reaching for the knob that turned on the sauna. There was the rattle of the old pipes deep in the walls, followed by the subtle hiss of the steam beginning to fill the redwood-lined chamber.

"So, were you a bad person in that room, specifically?" Aurora challenged gently. Again, her voice was irritatingly free of judgement. It was a pure exploration of Susan's thoughts. Aurora opened one of the linen cabinet doors and fetched Susan's favorite fluffy robe. She'd stolen it from a hotel she'd stayed in while on a work trip in Monaco.

Aurora extended the robe as she turned her back for Susan to disrobe. Susan briefly wondered if she needed to physically remove her clothes. She'd manifested them on. Could she manifest them off? She considered her body, and the warm glitter sensation once again prickled along her flesh that wasn't flesh. Her clothes were gone, replaced with a classically elegant bathing suit. Slipping her arms into the over-fluffed bathrobe, Susan felt a familiar easing of tension as she answered Aurora's question. Even without actual muscles, she felt an emotional tension that manifested as physical sensation.

"Preston would say I ruined his life, I think. Some of the others probably appreciated my having the lady-balls to say out loud what they already knew. I think a few of them even sued Preston and his buddies over that shit. I didn't get involved after I left that day though. It depends on who you ask, I guess."

"They did sue him for breach of contract and investor fraud as the company was employee-owned. They won. And I'm asking you, Susan," Aurora replied coolly. "Do you think you were a bad person in that room?"

"No. I don't think I was the bad person in that room. Crass, perhaps. But not the bad person. Or even *a* bad person. I was getting taken advantage of and then gaslit about it, and I stood up for myself."

"You did more than that, I think." Aurora observed, turning back to face Susan, a thin smile stretching her lips against her teeth and making her eyes crinkle at the corners. "You stood up for yourself, yes. But you also gave everyone in that room permission to stand up for themselves, as well."

"But I didn't really care about them or their ends. I cared that Preston save his breath and my time. I didn't need to haul his barrel of shit around if he was dumping us like cadavers in a river. It was a selfish motive. If someone else made something out of my leftovers, that doesn't impact whether I did it for good or for evil." Susan pulled open the door to the steam room and inhaled deeply as the warm, moist air brushed past her, caressing her cheeks with the familiarity of a seasoned lover.

"Oh." Aurora's hand flew to her mouth. "That's a new word."

Susan settled herself against the redwood panels of the steam room. Muscle memory activated and she started to reach out for the timer. As her fingers found the knob, exactly where her hand knew it would be, Susan wondered if it mattered how long she let herself simmer in the hot clouds. If time wasn't time, and she was more a puddle of energy and emotions than an actual person, it shouldn't matter at all how long she spent in there. She couldn't overheat, so what did it matter? "What? What's a new word?" Susan asked, letting her eyes falls closed and head loll back. Aurora had followed her into the steam room despite being fully clothed.

"Evil. So far, we've been trying to help you decide if Susan Chambers was a good or a bad person. But now you've gone and added a new level. You said for good or for evil."

"Those words are interchangeable. You know what I meant." Susan attempted to dismiss it. She hadn't meant anything by the word choice. It had just sort of slipped out.

"Are words interchangeable, Susan?" Aurora challenged. She didn't look even a little damp despite the hot fog.

"You would know, having spent this entire existence worrying with copy and text."

Susan's lips tightened, but Aurora was right. Good text could make up for mediocre graphic design. Bad copy would kill even the most impeccable imagery. Bad was one thing. But evil? Evil carried a much darker connotation.

Aurora clarified her question. "Do you think you were an evil person?"

Susan sighed. "No. Not evil. I had morals. I would sometimes ignore a few of the little ones, but I wouldn't murder someone or stand by while someone else got murdered in front of me. I was mean. I was cruel. I was selfish. I was a bad person. But I wasn't evil."

Aurora said nothing to this. She just watched, her eyes infuriatingly patient. Susan swallowed the full admission. She'd been a bad person. She did bad things. She'd known they were bad and conscientiously chose to do them anyway.

Maybe it was good a bike rack exposed her head meat to open air. If she'd ordered one more drink before leaving the restaurant, the bus would have missed her, and she would have continued sabotaging peers for a half inch of upward mobility, stepping on underlings like stepladders. She would have continued being awful to those around her unless they were useful to her. And even those people she would have discarded once she'd bled them dry, like a god-damned vampire. The realization sunk talons into her. Susan lifted her chin, attempting to accept it and move on. What was done was done. Her patience for this self-loathing shit was spent.

"Are we done here? Can we go to whatever part comes next?"

"No. We are not done here." Aurora's chipper sweetness had returned. Susan was typically impeccable at reading a person, but she couldn't quite get a bead on this guide to the afterlife. Or after death. Or whatever she called wherever they were. "I'd like to revisit something that happened here." Aurora gestured around her but frowned. "Well. Not here in the steam room, but in this house. The one you shared with Kevin."

"I don't know what else I'm supposed to gain from continuing to rehash this. I lived the life I lived. I was myself. I don't know that it matters if I was good or bad or evil or a fucking saint. I lived. I chose. I died. And I'm done with it now. I'll cross my fingers and hope I make less shitty, self-serving choices in the next life."

"Are you glad to be done living life as yourself?"

Susan took a moment to consider this question.

"No. I mean, of course not. I still had plans and goals and things I wanted to achieve. So much so that I was too engrossed in an email to notice an entire bus bearing down on me."

"If given the chance," Aurora held her hands up in that placating gesture again, "and I can't give you that chance, to be clear, but if given the chance, would you return to your life as Susan Chambers?"

Susan took a deep breath, letting her chest fully expand, and blew it back out. She was a bad person. But, still, she wasn't evil. Could a silk purse be made from a sow's ear? No. But a sow's ear could be turned into a damn decent clutch in the hands of the right craftsman.

"Yes. Absolutely. I would go back to my own life."

"Even though you think you were a bad person who made shitty, self-serving choices?" Aurora's left eyebrow seemed to be fighting a losing battle to stay down, instead lifting in a sardonic challenge.

Susan looked at her feet for several moments before lifting her head to make eye contact with Aurora.

"I think that this is my Dickensian moment. I think that you would be the ghosts, and I've had all the re-education. If I had the chance to go back to my life, I'd be the one telling the street urchin to buy the Christmas goose, and I'd give my Bob Cratchet a hearty raise. I think I was a bad person, but I'd try harder to be a good one with my second chance."

"Interesting," was all Aurora said.

"What does that mean?"

"It means I think that's an interesting observation, is all."

"Explain." Susan had accidentally reverted to what she called her boardroom voice, husky and commanding. The way Aurora's lips pursed at the command told Susan she was aware of that tone as well.

"You think that Susan Chambers was a bad person for her attitude, yes?"

"More for her selfishness. But that's splitting hairs, so, yes." Susan swallowed a lump that was rising in her throat.

"But you would willingly return to that life if you could, pick up where you left off, but this time trying harder to be a good person?"

Susan thought for a long time. Aurora had not so much as shifted a toe and displayed nothing but the pinnacle of patience when Susan finally said,

"Yes. If I could go back to that life, I would Ebenezer Scrooge the shit out of it."

"Interesting."

"What is interesting?" Susan ground out. "You keep clarifying instead of explaining." She was a little offended. She'd confidently said that yes, she would try to be a better person, and Aurora was being obtuse. It was selfish, but Susan wanted a little credit for what seemed like a major personal growth moment. And then Aurora shrugged.

That nonchalant, noncommittal wiggle of her shoulder lit a familiar little fire inside Susan's belly. She curled her hand up, expecting the tiny ache that normally accompanied a flare of annoyance.

"It just doesn't seem like a bad person would care about trying to be a good person. Or even care that they'd been perceived as a bad person. It seems to me that a bad person probably wouldn't have noticed they were bad," Aurora pronounced, her voice distant and slightly distracted, as if she were musing to herself, rather than speaking to Susan.

As her sentence ended, the steam picked up, growing from a misty veil to a heavy, impenetrable fog. Susan waved her hand through the haze, and as the cloud thinned and parted, she saw that she was no longer in her little cedar-lined haven. Instead, she was in the kitchen of the same house, but rather than Aurora sitting next to her, it was Kevin. Susan reached out for the spoon sitting next to the perfectly styled yogurt bowl before her and realized she'd not chosen to do that. She was a passenger in her own memory again, not in control of her body.

Kevin had been a creature of extreme habit. He woke at the same time every morning and went for a run, following the same five-mile path each day. After his hour run, he showered, dressed in a button-up and slacks, and fixed himself three eggs, half an avocado, his body weight in everything but the bagel seasoning, a hearty spoonful of probiotic pickled onions and a greens shake that Susan always thought tasted like grass clippings drowned in salt water that had been shown an interpretive dance about the fruit medley it was supposed to taste like.

He was in advertising, like her, but he was a numbers guy, not a creative type. Susan's job was to tap into the human psyche and convince folks they needed whatever it was Susan was selling. Kevin was the guy who looked at who consumed the ad, how many units were moved or actions taken, and decided whether the campaign was successful. He used words that weren't words to do this, and Susan hated when Kevin talked shop.

"When Alex realized these absolute morons never made the shift from B2B-centered KPIs, I about ripped someone's head off. How the fuck did they not notice? The bounce rate was off the charts and conversion rate was negative. Like, how do you even manage a negative conversion rate?" Kevin only required Susan's presence for these rants. Not her participation. She ate her breakfast in a stupor. "And what the hell happened to the A/B metrics that no one fuck- ing noticed they weren't speaking a B2C language?" Susan purposefully shoved a granola-heavy bite of her yogurt bowl into her mouth, hoping the crunching would drown her husband out. "Of course, they're gonna churn the minute a CTA doesn't make sense. It's apples and oranges, babe. German and Chinese. We don't cross the streams, Ray. Buyer personas are disengaging, but the RPM is scaled to industry jargon instead of consumer trends."

"Fuck, Kevin. It's too early for acronyms. Can you just say the words? You sound like a child learning their ABCs in the wrong order." The words were out of Susan's mouth before her sleep-addled brain could stop them. Kevin's fork clattered to the plate with more force than gravity alone could have managed. Susan flinched. Fuck. She hated that she flinched so damn much.

"Oh. I'm sorry." Kevin was speaking slowly, drawing each syllable through his teeth. "My fault. My stupid little wife needs me to slow it down. Were all the letters too much for your itty-bitty brain this morning, babe?" Susan felt the practiced expression scratch itself across her features. Soft eyes, lowered lashes, lick your lips. Look contrite. Deescalate.

Susan's hand shot out and grasped the coffee mug, tugging it protectively in front of her face. The ceramic was hot, and her fingertips felt like they were welding to the cup, but she didn't let the pain show. Kevin tended to avoid anything that would get him messy too, and hot coffee was normally an excellent deterrent.

"I'm sorry, hon," Susan demurred. "You know how I get before my coffee." Kevin looked at her then, the full bore of his gaze made every muscle in her body brace. She held that gaze as she took a committed sip of the coffee. She could feel the molten heat slide all the way down her chest as she swallowed. She willed her face to stay neutral. If he sensed she was uncomfortable, he'd go even deeper. But it was too late. He'd gotten to the edge of his tolerance and dove off.

Susan hadn't even seen him wind up. Kevin's fist connected with that mug of coffee and her caffeinated shield splattered the room. It hit Susan's yogurt bowl as it flew. While the yogurt splashed away from her, sparing her blouse from the spirulina dying it blue, most of the coffee landed in her lap. She felt the blisters bloom instantly but refused to let her expression betray her. He could not know of her pain. He might like it and start hurting her intentionally.

Susan knew she had to give credit where credit was due. Lots of things were shattered in his fits, but Kevin never actually struck Susan. The only injuries his tantrums yielded were collateral damage. A broken dish, but never a broken nose. A few blisters from hot coffee striped her thighs, but she never endured handprint-shaped bruises or twisting fractures. She knew if she kept calm and avoided eye contact, her husband would scream some more but then take himself to work. It would all be forgotten by dinner.

"No." Kevin shook his head, his hands pressed down on the marble so hard, Susan would not have been surprised to see indents left behind when he lifted his white-knuckled fists. "Coffee doesn't fix snooty, you uppity bitch." Kevin closed the distance between them in the blink of an eye. "What? You think you're the queen of fuck all because you're above using acronyms? Letters too baby-ish for you?"

His hand wrapped itself around the back of Susan's skull, holding her in place a hair's breadth from his face. His volume jumped to ear-splitting volume as he roared, "You think you're fucking better than me?! Is that what this is about?!" Kevin turned as he shoved her head forward. Susan made a note to thank her Pilates teacher for all that core work they'd been doing. Those ab workouts had given her just enough control to stop her face from impacting the marble, with a solid inch to spare.

As Susan righted herself, Kevin was already halfway out of the kitchen. "I'm sorry to have inconvenienced you with my immaturity, Susan," he spat over his shoulder. "I'll take myself to nursery school to finish learning my fuck-ing ABCs." Susan stayed perfectly still through a clatter of keys and a crashing of glass, likely the little plate that held their keys and pocket sundries being pitched across the foyer. She didn't move until the front door slammed, and then Susan endured the distinct sensation of all the air being sucked out of the room.

Her chest calcified itself while her diaphragm forgot how to move. Bones began vibrating under her skin, fine cracks webbing through them so when they shook themselves apart, a million pieces would fall. Muscles pulled themselves in every direction all at once. Her stomach felt like it was turning inside out. Her brain started ripping parts of itself off and throwing those hunks of grey matter at the inside of her skull. She could stop this. She could end this part. There was a word. An important word that would make her safe again. It would give her air. But words were out of reach. Words were less important than air. Air. How did she get air? Her vision started pulsing black and blue at the edges. Her hand throbbed arrhythmically at her side. Hot then cool. Cool and then cold. Heat roared next, skin bubbling, her hand a frozen fire. Susan had just opened her mouth trying to dislodge the silent scream obscuring her airway when Aurora was beside her, one small-boned hand on Susan's arm. "You don't need air. You don't have a body."

Just as suddenly as the panic attack attempted to take hold, it stopped. All the alarm bells and air raid sirens in Susan's body silenced. "Sorry," she said reflexively.

"There's no need to apologize. Panic attacks were a common part of your life in that period. I'm not surprised one tried to trigger." Aurora offered. Aurora walked over to the espresso machine to their left and fired it up. The machine hummed and whined as it did its work. "Walk me through what that was." Susan heard Aurora's question, but she was staring at her hand. Her fingers looked fine, but back when the memory had been playing out the first time, her fingertips had been so viciously red that Susan wondered if she had burned off her own fingerprints clutching that coffee. And for nothing, too. Though she knew the blisters weren't there, she ran a hand across the leggings wrapping her thighs anyway.

"That was my ex-husband at his worst." Susan announced. "He had a temper."

"That was just a temper?" Aurora confirmed, sliding a simple white cup under the drip spout of the espresso machine.

"For Kevin, it was. He was easily triggered." Susan shrugged. Her mercifully unscorched fingertip had begun tracing a dark swirl across the marble counter.

A clatter resonated through the kitchen and Susan screamed, despite herself. Aurora had dropped a spoon. That panic attack had receded, but only just. "Sorry!" This apology came out less reflexively, dripping with frustration instead.

"No. My apologies. You're still jumpy, and I was careless." Aurora countered, turning to lean her hip against the coffee bar. She clasped her hands just under her bust, one hand wiggling the offending spoon back and forth. "I did notice you just defended your ex-husband to me. That's interesting."

Susan chuckled. "Habit, I suppose. I spent quite a bit of time defending my ex-husband to most of my family, friends, coworkers, and acquaintances."

"Yes. I see that. But why did you feel the need to keep defending him?"

Susan opened her mouth to answer but stopped short of saying the words. She wasn't sure what words to say. The espresso machine churned merrily as it dispensed milk in the fresh brew. Susan had insisted Kevin buy her the absolute pinnacle of home espresso machines. It was as close as she could get to her beloved Italian espresso in between her annual visits to the country.

She'd never had issues convincing Kevin to buy her the things she wanted. All it took was waiting for him to lose his temper. After his customary apology fuck, he'd feel bad for his outburst and buy her something nice to assuage his guilt. At least half her shoe collection, a third of her watches, every strand of pearls she owned, and that espresso machine had been paid for by Kevin's temper.

"Susan. You're dead. Your story has been written, approved, and sent to press." Aurora spoke slowly, as if pitching a bold idea to a hesitant client. "No matter what you think or say about him now, he can't hurt you."

"You know, you say a lot of insightful things. Does that stuff just come to you, or…?" Susan trailed off and watched Aurora expectantly. Her guide's impeccably impartial expression sank just a bit. Aurora's eyebrows furrowed and her eyes narrowed. But when she replied, her voice was just as even as before.

"I'm an old soul. Lots of experience with insightful things. Probably. I, like you, don't remember my past lives. But my soul was old enough to become a guide, so I must have lived a life or seven thousand." Aurora shrugged. "And I noticed you trying to switch topics." Susan chuckled at that. "Allow me to direct us back to the topic at hand. Do you still think you were a bad person?"

"Yes." Susan paused for effect. "And no." It was Aurora's turn to chuckle. "I think I did bad things, but I don't think I ever set out to hurt anyone in the doing of them. I think I married a man who was a lot like me but more open about it."

The espresso had been transformed into a latte by Susan's favorite tantrum apology gift. Aurora carried the cup over to Susan, who still perched on the criminally uncomfort-able barstool. Susan hugged the cup with her hands but did not take a drink—the memory of sipping the too-hot coffee still rankled a bit. "Everyone who knew Kevin accepted that he had a temper and was prone to outbursts. It wasn't a surprise when he lashed out. He would hurt people's feelings or sabotage their projects just to prove he could. It was a way to show those around him that he was the power player. He was the one in charge."

"Was Kevin a bad person?" Aurora tipped forward and rested her forearms on the bar. She looked relaxed but still attentive.

"It's not my place to pass judgment on someone else." Susan dismissed her guide's question as she stared into the milk foam. Aurora scoffed.

"This may sound impertinent, but it absolutely is your place to pass judgment. Kevin was a part of your life. His choices shaped some of yours. His actions defined parts of your path." Aurora chided. "You are allowed to judge people where their lives intersect with yours. Perhaps in life, there's something to be said for discretion in who you communicate that with, if you tell anyone at all," she shrugged a cream-clad shoulder, "but the idea that you can't judge people for the impact they had on your life is a little silly. Judge away, Susan."

Susan sat the cup down. It made a clink against the marble. Susan's voice came out softer than intended.

"Yes. I think Kevin was a bad person." Susan had expected the proclamation to taste bad or sit heavy or sting as she said it. But it didn't. It felt good to admit, out loud, that she thought her ex-husband was a bad person. Kevin had been a bad husband, a bad coworker, a bad boss, and a bad man. Susan felt the soft, safe edges of relief begin to take hold of her. Until another realization doused her like ice water.

Kevin had been a bad man. And she'd had married him. Even worse, for a brief period, she had loved him. Susan lifted her eyes from her coffee to Aurora's gaze. Aurora blinked, patiently waiting for Susan to parse through her past. "I loved a bad person. That can't say good things about me."

"Did you love him because he was bad?" Aurora's challenge was gentle.

"No."

"Did you realize he was bad when you loved him?"

Susan almost said yes but halted herself. That relief started to slip back around Susan. "No. I didn't see him for what he was until later." She'd known what Kevin was like in the corporate world, but while they dated, he'd shown nothing of that side of him to her in his personal life. That cutthroat in Kevin had been reserved for the boardrooms he operated in. With Susan, he'd been sweet, patient, attentive, and kind until a few months after their wedding. About the time Kevin started showing his true colors, sleeping with whomever he pleased, and being generally despicable to Susan was about the time she fell out of love with the man.

Aurora lifted herself to upright, her hands finding their customary spot clasped between her hip bones. "Did loving him make you a bad person by association?"

Susan let her head fall to the side, considering the question. She chewed on her lower lip while she pondered. Plenty of good people fell for the wrong person. She'd known more than her fair share of lovely people with atrocious taste in partners.

"Opposites attract, but so too do birds of a feather." Susan explained as she let her finger circle the edge of the coffee cup. "We ended up together because we were very similar. Kevin hurt feelings and tanked goals. So did I. I was sneakier about the pain I inflicted. For Kevin, it was about power. He hurt people to prove a point. For me, it was about control. I didn't hurt people if I didn't have to. If I could move them without destroying them, I'd do that. But I wouldn't hesitate to annihilate their entire career if the ends justified the means."

"Like you did with Christine Caldwell?" Aurora offered.

"Like I did with Christine Caldwell," Susan confirmed. "Not everyone was that lucky. Not everyone I had to move to keep in control of the situation came out the victor. But I did try to keep the collateral damage to a minimum. It was a conscious effort on my part."

"You made a conscious effort to save those you could?"

" 'Save' is maybe too strong a word. 'Spare' might work better. I spared who I could, sometimes actively like Christine, sometimes by just ignoring them."

"Is that something a bad person does, Susan?" Aurora looked like she was fighting every muscle in her face to keep it from grinning.

"I'd say that lands me more in the 'selfish bitch' category. Maybe not all the way into bad-person-land, though." Susan acquiesced. "You don't look convinced."

"I'm not the one that needs convincing. This is your soul and your life, not mine. Do you feel like being a selfish bitch, if not a bad person, is what your soul learned from your life as Susan Chambers?"

"I honestly don't know. I don't really know what my soul should learn from this."

"Well, what have you learned since waking up here?"

"That I was a selfish bitch, have been since middle school, and my ex-husband was a twat-waffle." That came out a touch more derisive than Susan had meant it to.

"You already knew that, even if you've never said the words out loud." Aurora replied. Susan felt her brows knit together defensively, but she smoothed them back out, realizing Aurora was right. Again. That was getting kind of old, Aurora being right.

In life, Susan knew she was a selfish bitch. She often prided herself at the back half of that moniker. Susan Chambers was the bitchiest bitch ever to bitch. The 'selfish' part, though, she'd spent quite a bit of time shoving that acknowledgment deep into the dark corners of her self-consciousness.

Aurora took a deep breath and her eyes drifted upward and stayed there. After an abnormally long pause, she said, "Okay, we're going to try something here. I've seen this done just the once, so be patient with me while I figure out this interface." Her eyes were still cast to the ceiling as she spoke, and the kitchen faded away.

It was replaced with a conference room. Not the horrid yellow and black, preteen-wet-dream one of Coconut Express. This one was sleek, elegant, adult, and back-dropped with a stunning view of the Empire State Building. The full glass wall was polished to crystal-clear perfection.

Susan recognized this because she had insisted it be so, regularly and with emphasis. She'd gone so far as to learn how to complain about streaks and fingerprints in Span-ish, as the cleaning crew all hailed from the Dominican Republic. It wasn't truly her conference room. It belonged to Abernathy Ad Executives, the company Susan had been VP of when she died. She had an entire office, but it was on the other side of the floor. Thus, it looked out over the bustling street below and then the boring brown wall of their nearest sky-scraping neighbor.

Susan set up camp in the conference room often, just for that view. Hence, she encouraged the cleaning crew to put a little extra oomph in their cleaning of that glass. She secured that oomph by leaving a crisp portrait of Benjamin Franklin done in stunning shades of green in the cleaning closet, tucked around the spray bottle labeled *Limpiador de Ventanas*. Sure enough, either the bitching or the bribery ensured that those conference room windows were always spotless and streak-free.

The conference room table was clean, save Susan's trusty laptop and cellphone.

Gasping, Susan darted over to it. Without thinking, she grabbed the phone and held it to her chest. She somehow felt complete with the device in hand.

"Is it strange to say I feel better holding this thing?" Susan asked her guide.

"No. Not at all." Aurora clarified. "For much of your adult life, you were dependent on your phone. It's not odd to feel a certain amount of safety with the object that demanded so much of your attention."

Susan nodded. Once, she'd stormed into a meeting of the IT department and demanded they help her immediately. Her phone had locked up and was basically a brick. Susan hadn't felt that frightened even while Kevin was threatening her with real violence. Her entire career was tied to that phone.

Frank, the IT Head, had taken one look and asked her when the last time she'd updated it had been. Susan could only shrug. It had taken the man thirty-two seconds to fix whatever had gone wrong. When he returned her phone, all her apps and services functioning as normal, she'd nearly cried with relief. Susan couldn't remember if she'd said thank you to him. She probably hadn't.

Susan looked up at Aurora, who'd resumed that patient watching thing she did. "Sorry, lost in my thoughts."

"No apologies. That's kind of the point. Think those thoughts. Let yourself get lost in them. Think anything important?"

"I don't know if it's important. But I was thinking of a time I needed help, someone helped me, and that I don't think I said 'Thank you.' "

"And that bothers you?"

"Well, yeah. I didn't say thank you. That's bad. It's a thing bad people do. Especially when I knew better. I was taught, by rod and by rote memorization, all my manners. Especially the pleases and the thank yous."

"And you feel bad for not using those manners after someone helped you?" Aurora's voice flipped up as the question finished. Susan felt annoyance burble and burp in her chest.

"Yes. Why did you phrase that as a question?" Susan was incredulous. "Of course, I feel bad I was a dick to someone. I feel worse that I didn't notice until after I literally died."

"Who taught you those manners? 'By rod and by rote memorization.' " Aurora parroted Susan's words back to her.

"Oh, my saint of mother made sure I knew how to be the most perfect little lady to ever exist, come hell or highwater." Susan had let her voice fall flat. There was no reason pretending, especially after her own demise, that she had any appreciation for her mother's choices in parenthood. Elizabeth had been the product of bad choices and problem resolution by way of abject violence. Susan's mother swore up and down that her family were not mafia grunts, but no one believed her. One look at the menfolk of the family and you just knew these Dorito-shaped boys were genetically designed to be someone's muscle.

Elizabeth had grown up with a father who worked sporadically and drank reliably. Her mother, Susan's grandmother, worked to the bone at a hundred different jobs to keep them in a small apartment in the Bronx. When that drunken man eventually wandered away, likely in a stupor and didn't return, neither Elizabeth nor Susan's grandmother truly felt his absence. Susan's mother didn't talk much about her childhood. It was uncouth, and what happened in the past should stay in the past. What Susan did know was that the moment her mother had turned eighteen, she fled the Bronx, all the way up to Bangor, Maine.

She found herself a trust-fund baby and settled into life as a trophy wife. They had themselves four children, first Samuel, and then Susan. Finally came the twins, but they came too early. Susan was only five when her too-little sisters were born. They survived all of three hours in their plastic boxes before passing away. Susan didn't remember her mother before the twins came and went, but her older brother did. He said something broke inside their mother's soul.

Now, armed with a new understanding of the nature of souls, Susan wondered if that were true. "Can a soul be broken?" Susan asked. Aurora's face fell slightly, just for a moment.

"Yes. They can."

"What breaks them?" Susan felt an insatiable need to understand this.

"A lot of things. Just as in your most recent experience as Susan Chambers, people have different catalysts to absolute collapse. A soul's breaking point can be a lot of things or just one big, horrid experience."

"What happens? When a soul breaks?"

"Different things. Sometimes they heal. Sometimes they work through how much of the bad that happened in their last existence wasn't their fault. Sometimes they choose their next existence very thoughtfully, looking for something that promises to be easy and comforting. And sometimes…" Aurora's voice trailed off. Her eyes looked sad, wounded, even.

"Sometimes…" Susan prompted. Aurora let out a long exhale.

"Sometimes they break so deeply, they can't put themselves together again. Sometimes the wounds sustained
from hardship, torture, and struggle are so gaping, the
soul just stops. They don't cycle, or reincarnate, as
you'd call it. They sit with the memories of the life
that broke them until they fade, crumble, and dissolve
away."

"Wouldn't that take trillion and trillions of years?"

"Occasionally, yes. But for the most part, once a soul has
reached that horrid place of being that very hurt, they fade
much faster."

"What happens to a soul after it fades?"

"Nothing. It just stops being." Aurora said this the same
way someone might say water is wet or the sun is bright.

"Nothing? That's it?" Susan felt a little let down by that.

"That's it. All things must end. Souls will cycle through
hundreds of thousands of versions of existence until one
day they reach the end of what they need to know. Unfathomable amounts of experiences, sensation, thoughts, and
feelings were gathered from their vast lifespan and many
iterations and attempts at a life lived. At the end of it all,
they can look back and understand what it was to exist,
and then they stop doing that. Existing. It was enough.
They figured it out."

Susan felt deeply conflicted by this, but she couldn't figure out why. "They figure out the meaning of life and then stop living it?"

"In a sense, yeah." Aurora nodded encouragingly. "The point of living is to figure out the point of living." Aurora paused and cocked her head. "You're bothered by this."

"A little, but I don't know why. I don't know what I expected. It makes perfect sense, but it also feels wasteful. You finally figure it all out, and then just poof out of existence. I don't know. It's giving me this nihilistic feeling that honestly would hurt my brain if I still had one. If figuring out the point is the whole point, what's the point?" Susan shook her head. It felt so inane to say it out loud like that.

"That's because you're still young—your soul is. You have a lot of questions you haven't even thought of asking yet. It feels pointless because you have so many more things to discover. I hate to sound this way, but it's one of those things you can't understand until you're ready to understand." Aurora flicked her eyes upward again and then right back down. "Let's put a pin in this and discuss why we are here in your conference room."

"It's not my conference room, technic—"

"It's your conference room." Aurora interjected. "After your death, they named it after you."

Susan felt like someone had attacked her with a bat for the blow that landed. They named her conference room after her. "Like, in memoriam?"

"Yep. In Memoriam. The Susan Chambers Conference Room. Your company wanted to honor all the work you'd done for them by attaching your name to the place in which you did so much of that tremendous work."

"But I thought they all hated me."

"What gave you that impression?" Aurora had flipped back into that therapist voice. It rankled on Susan.

"You! *You* gave me that impression. All that chatter about what people think of me and how they perceived me." Her frustration was rising with every word. She would have been panting, but Susan had finally figured out the body/no body relationship and knew she didn't need air, so panting was pointless, and a tad melodramatic.

"I told you how people perceived you. You decided the connotation of those feelings."

"Oh, we're back to this game."

"It's not a game. It's a part of the process," Aurora said as she lifted her hand, extending her index finger and selecting something from mid-air. Susan blinked and they were no longer alone in the room.

Right next to Aurora was her mother, Elizabeth Elaine Mason Chambers, aged around forty. Susan's knowledge of the body/no body relationship absented itself, and now Susan was panting. The panting turned to crying, which turned to sobbing. Aurora approached and threw her arms out as Susan's knees buckled. Elizabeth only watched. So on brand for her. As moans and wails scratched their way out of Susan's throat, the shock waned to frustration. Within moments, she was in a full rage. Disentangling her limbs from Aurora's, Susan flew to her feet and was across the room in less than moments.

Reaching her mother, Susan planted both hands on her chest and shoved as hard as she could. Elizabeth stumbled backward, but her face didn't change, nor did she fall. She righted herself and continued looking placid and judgmental. Aurora was still crouched on the floor where Susan had rejected her attempt at comfort. Susan made a series of spluttering sounds she wasn't completely sure the intended meaning of.

"It's a representation of your mother. Not your actual mother. An illusion, but an important one." Aurora's voice floated up from the floor.

"Why?" Susan growled. The rage was consuming her. It burned deep, charring through the scars and mottled bits of flesh that held parts of Susan together. She felt raw, exposed.

"Because you still believe you're a bad person despite what you tried to get me to believe. Because you've internalized so much of what she did to you." Aurora's hand lifted again. Another finger poked empty space. The crowd grew: Kevin appeared, just as alertly blank as her mother. "Or what he did to you." Another person joined them. One of Susan's old bosses, James Katz. The first man to give her real power by handing her a division head position, as well as the first man to demonstrate just how quickly he could render her powerless. "Or him."

The conference room almost shimmered. When Susan blinked, it had become a tennis court. The windows had been replaced with high, kelly-green walls topped with chain-link fence. The net stretched across the center of the court, a brilliant blue splash across a red clay sea. Susan felt the familiar grip of her tennis racket, her fingers aching for how hard she was clutching it. Her skirt ruffled in the breeze, and she reached behind her to prevent the back from blowing up, but another hand reached the fabric first.

"Even the wind knows what's good for us, Ms. Chambers." James' voice was too close to her ear. She could smell the tobacco on his breath. James claimed he didn't smoke, but the tiny brown patch on his Tom Selleck mustache betrayed him. His hand smoothed the skirt back down, gliding slowly over the swell of her ass and lingering. Susan took a big step forward, pivoting to face him.

"Mm. The wind is telling me you're afraid you're about to get beat by a lowly department head, sir." Susan's voice was higher than her normal speaking voice, her tone buoyant. She ignored the nausea. That part was easy. Constantly guessing and then avoiding where James wanted to put his hands was the difficult part.

"Oh, I'm not about to get beat by a lowly department head." Susan arched her eyebrow the way she knew he liked. "I'm about to get beat by a Junior Executive Director." Susan's mouth fell open and she didn't bother to close it.

"You're promoting me?" Susan said, forgetting to modulate her voice so it came out deeper and huskier than she'd meant.

"Depends on what happens next." James winked as he spoke, his voice dropping. His eyes were hooded, darker. Susan backed up half a step. James responded with a full step, closing the gap between them.

"Oh, I'll throw this game if you'd like. I'll throw this game and tell everyone at the office you pounded me to the ground." Susan's gut churned, flooded with regret for her word choice. James' chin dipped and his breath sawed out of him. Flicking his tongue out to lick his lips, his eyes slipped down her body. She could feel his gaze squirm up and down her, spending too long on her breasts and even longer still at her crotch. She ignored the slimy feeling pooling in her limbs.

"Pounding would be a good finale. But I'm not going to make it a condition of your promotion. That would be unethical." Another step forward and Susan could feel the heat rolling off his body. Every cell in her body screamed at her, but she stood her ground, refusing to flinch. Her flinching days were behind her. She needed this, and she was a woman who did what needed to be done. She would do what needs must. "But if you're willing to incentivize me just a bit, maybe that raise will be just as generous as the title."

James arched his back subtly, ruffling the edge of her skirt with the evidence of his arousal. Every muscle in Susan's mid-section clenched painfully. A familiar ache bloomed across her hand, an old anxiety flaring in Susan's body. James' hand rose to her shoulder, one finger landing at her collar bone. It traced swirling patterns across the thin skin there and doodled a path back down her arm. The trail ended at her wrist when he gently grabbed it and guided it toward his bright yellow shorts.

"Aardvark."

Susan was back in the boardroom, facing James, Kevin, and Elizabeth. "You're a bitch, Aurora." Susan ground out. "You're a fucking bitch." Susan wanted to cry. She wanted to curl up and sleep for days. She wanted to hit something.

"I know you feel that way, Susan." Aurora's voice betrayed nothing. Neither remorse, nor pity.

Susan emptied entirely then. Where rage burned and roiled and consumed, an icy numbness picked through the burn scars and blackened landscape of her insides. Her breathing didn't just level, it stopped. She didn't need air and she didn't need Aurora and she didn't need this. "This is cruel." Susan's voice rasped out in a shredded whisper.

"I am sorry. But we were doing a little spinning and settling." Aurora replied. She gestured to Susan's tormentors. "These people victimized you. They used, abused, and harmed you through their words, their actions, and their inactions. You spent this entire iteration of your soul's existence trying to rectify their badness, to settle accounts with the damage they left on you."

"Nothing they ever did to me justifies me making it everyone else's problem!" Susan was shouting but didn't care to stop. "My trauma is not a justification for being an asshole. I was miserable. Sure. But I never had the right to make everyone else miserable as a result!" Every fiber of her being threatened to tear itself apart. She was a bad person. She did bad things. "How can you not see that, Aurora? What are you trying to fish out of me? Susan Chambers was mean and petty purely because she could be. My mother, my ex-husband, my wanker of a boss, they were my tutors in being a bad person. But their lessons did not exonerate me from making different choices once I was out from under their thumbs and their control!"

Aurora did not cower. She simply curled her legs up, lowering herself from a crouch to a princess sit, her ankles crossed and tucked beside one hip. Her skirt stretched taut across her thighs, and she smoothed it with her hands. Susan thought her guide was vibrating slightly until she realized Aurora was still. Susan was trembling. Aurora tipped her head, one edge of her soft bob waving gently.

She said nothing.

Susan said nothing.

For a long time.

Hours. Or months. Or centuries. Susan didn't know how time worked. Susan didn't care.

The pair stared at each other.

Aurora's voice was a sweet caress when she finally slipped her words through the silence that had extended between them. "You were not a bad person, Susan. You were not bad. You were wounded. These three forged all their brokenness into blades. They honed them with their own trauma and used you like a pin cushion, ramming their insecurities, rage, and fear into you." Aurora paused, her eyes boring into Susan. She licked her lips before continuing.

"You carried those blades like a burden. They kept your wounds open and festering. Every time you even thought to nurse them, the blades would open those wounds anew. And every time, it hurt. You couldn't begin to heal." Susan wanted to curl up into the fetal position. She wanted to retch. She wanted this to stop. She wanted to slap her mother. Instead, she stayed still. "Say it." Aurora issued the command. "Say what you're thinking."

Susan blinked. Her eyes slowly tracked across the three figures that stood watching her watch them, their faces neutral, their hands just dangling at their sides.

She took in Kevin, and even though she knew it was little more than an image, it had captured the dull look behind his eyes perfectly. He had never seen one inch in front of his own nose in his entire miserable existence. He was always in his head, living out delusions of grandeur. If it felt good, it was good, and so he pursued it. He pursued Susan, and once he had her, the thrill went out of it. It was the chase that kept his little cock plump. Once he caught his prey and satisfied his curiosity, he cast it aside. Susan felt it happen. She felt the shift. He was on a knee on top of a goddamn mountain and Susan watched his interest melt away under the heat of starlight. And she put that stupid ring on anyway. When Kevin got bored, he got bitter and took it out on Susan.

Next to him was James. She'd worked for James Katz for six years. All six of those years, he made her feel small.

Every time he grabbed her hand under the conference room table and put it on his crotch, he made her shrink just a little. Every time he put his dry, tobacco-stained-and-scented lips on her body, she diminished even more. Susan hated feeling small. To combat this, she doubled her work. She threw more of herself into perfecting the copy, selecting the perfect colorway, and pushing designers and formatters to absolute, unachievable perfection. And still felt small.

Finally, she got to her mother. Kevin and James' simulates kept their head on a steady, human-looking swivel as if they were taking in the room for the first time, absorbing details, silently understanding. But since Aurora had manifested this woman in the conference room with them, Elizabeth had not taken her eyes off Susan. Her mother's gaze bored through Susan's soul, exactly as it had done in life.

The conference room dissolved away and was replaced by a tiny little church sanctuary. Rows of maroon-cushioned pews marched away from Susan, who was sat on a shiny black piano bench, her fingers poised over the black and white planks. Susan sucked in air and tried to clench her fists to yank them away from the keyboard. But she was a passenger. "No!" Susan tried to yell. Her left hand. Her left hand was positioned wrong! No. Maman would see. She would know. But seven-year-old Susan didn't notice. They lowered to the keys and a discordant clank hammered out of the baby grand. Susan's stomach clenched, flipping over and over itself. Maman was going to be so sad. She'd yell and cry and scream. No. Stupid, stupid girl.

"Aardvark." Susan tried. Nothing happened. "Aardvark." Again, with emphasis. "Please, Aurora. Aardvark. Aardvark. AARDVARK!" Susan was begging, screaming in her mind to be released. She didn't have it in her to care that she sounded small or pitiful or pathetic. "No. Please. Don't make me watch this." Susan hadn't forgotten this memory. She didn't need to see it again. She didn't want to. Aurora was silent. No response. No change. The piano droned on.

She continued her pleading. "Please, no. Please, Aurora." The words came out broken, as if she were crying. "Aardvark. Please. Make it stop. I don't want it." But Susan wasn't crying. She was seven years old, playing the piano. "I'm sorry. Please. I am so sorry." Susan, young and old together, sobbed as her small, delicate fingers jerkily bounced across the keys, plucking out a tortuous Ode to Joy. The fucking irony. The music faded, as did the piano. Susan was in her living room, her mother, animated this time, standing in front of her.

"That was unacceptable, *mademoiselle*," Maman breathed.

The French. She always used French when she was going to do the worst things.

Susan's mother produced a dowel rod from behind her back. One of the heavy ones they used to prop the windows open with on hot summer days. "Hold your hands out so I can help you remember where to put them next time we play, *mon petit échec*," came Elizabeth's request. Susan held her hands out. They didn't even shake this time. They were so small. So soft. She'd been so young then. Susan felt a swell of pride eddy through her at how still she kept her hands while her mother lifted the dowel high above her head. The rod whistled as it sliced through the air. The skin of her knuckle cracked. A crushing sting zipped up Susan's arm. Another whipping blow and her hand felt like it melted. Hot and cold fought a war under her child's flesh. Waves of fire charred tendons and spikes of ice snapped bones. Susan's performance earned her a broken hand. It was no less than she deserved. She knew better and would not forget again.

She would not forget.

She never forgot.

The living room faded away, leaving a once again grown Susan cradling her hand. She risked flexing her fingers, bracing for pain that didn't come.

"Unacceptable." Susan ground out, the words shaping themselves around the quaver in her voice.

"What was unacceptable?" Aurora sounded far away, as if they were under water.

"The child at the piano hitting the wrong notes."

"No." Aurora's tone wasn't harsh. It was heavy but gentle. Grounded. "Try again."

"The child at the piano."

"No." That was almost a purr. "Oh, no—Susan…" Or was it a growl? Something lashed out and coiled around the base of Susan's spine. It clawed through her guts, spearing for her arm. It was violently hot and made her hand ache.

Fear.

Susan was afraid.

She forced herself to turn her head and look at Aurora. Her face was relaxed save a tiny crease between her brows. That could be an expression of concern. Or perhaps anger? Susan couldn't tell. She always needed to be able to tell or she might make it worse. A small part of Susan begged to take a step back. Distance herself from what she couldn't read. Give herself time to decide how to fix this, how to protect herself. Before Susan could decide how to gain control of the situation, Aurora spoke.

"It wasn't the child. It wasn't anything the child did. You know that, Susan Chambers. You've just never given yourself permission to say it. Try. Again." Aurora's words were clipped, dripping with more of that sacrosanct patience. "What was unacceptable?"

Susan looked down at her left hand. The scar from the surgery had faded from view by the time she was a teenager. But if she pressed her index finger just to the right of the single freckle near her wrist, she'd feel the bundle of scar tissue just under the surface, hard and unforgiving. That scar had been an important part of Susan, a constant reminder of the cost of failure.

"The mother." Susan was only capable of whispering this truth. It was too frightening to say it any louder. "The mother was unacceptable. She put the child at that piano and then broke the child." Susan thought she'd freeze solid where she stood. No more fire. No more burning. Let the fear and pain and regret drop her further and further into the icy depths of a boundless void.

"She did." Aurora whispered back. "She broke that little girl. She broke her skin. She broke her bones. She broke her spirit, and with everything in you, Susan, you tried to hold those broken bits together."

Susan took a step closer to her mother. Her core was trembling, but she couldn't tell if it was from fear or from anger. Another step and she willed herself to speak.

"Fuck you, Lizzy." Susan managed to stumble over the words, her body that wasn't a body physically lurching with force of the them leaving her lips. Her mother's name came out of her like a slur. "Fuck you, you self-righteous whore." A part of Susan's mind detached entirely from reality. She had the sensation of floating above herself, the instinctual part of Susan's soul an observer to this interaction, the perceptive part of her gainining momentum as the words flowed like a flooding river cresting its banks. "I was a child. Of course I messed up. Children mess up. They don't know. You're supposed to teach them, not punish for not knowing. Of course I cried. Children cry, you stupid bitch. It wasn't weakness. It was pain. And you thought you were the only one entitled to hurting."

Susan wasn't screaming. Her voice shredded itself through her teeth. "So, I learned to cram it down and to do it hurt. I wanted to give you whatever you needed. I needed to fix every bit of you so you'd be happy. You were so ashamed of your broken home and all those black eyes your daddy gave you that you thought the only answer to that was absolute fucking perfection!"

Susan couldn't stop the onslaught of everything all at once. "Perfect manners. Perfect dresses. Perfect speech. Perfect talent. Perfect child. You treated me like a doll you hated. You dressed me up and paraded me around and made me perform for all you and Daddy's friends. I was perfect for you. I WAS FUCKING PERFECT BECAUSE YOU NEEDED ME TO BE PERFECT!" Susan took a shaky breath.

"It wasn't enough. You didn't notice. You just kept pushing, pushing, pushing. Because no matter how perfect I was, it didn't make you any less broken. It was never going to be enough. You were supposed to teach me how to sur-vive. I didn't need to be broken to learn that." Susan was sobbing now but couldn't remember when the tears had started.

"What did you need, Susan?"

"I needed support. I needed love. She was too lost in her own pain to give me those things. She was broken, and that's all she knew. That's all she knew, so she broke me."

"That sounds familiar." Aurora took a single step toward her. The conference room was gone. They were in a room. Non-descript. Non-threatening. It looked like a waiting room, but for something you *wanted* to wait for. Aurora slipped just a hair's breadth closer, extending her hand toward Susan. "A broken person try-ing to break others so all her shattered pieces would feel less alone."

"Oh, fuck me." Susan's knees buckled and she was on all fours, hands sprawled across unfamiliar linoleum flooring. "I was doing it too. I was doing…" Aurora was beside her, one hand on her back, the other hand laid one gentle fin-ger across Susan's lips, shushing her rather than silencing.

"You were doing what you were taught to do. But you were also trying to be better." Susan was surprised at the strength in Aurora's embrace. It wasn't clinging, it was supporting. "Without guidance, without counseling, without someone to point out just how deep those knife wounds went, you were trying to be *more* than you were taught to be." Susan forced herself to tear her eyes off the trailing splotches of color dribbled across the tiles. When she lifted her head, Aurora's face was right there, inches from hers. "You weren't a bad person."

Despite herself, Susan still felt silly for the sniffle that escaped her. She rolled her eyes. She'd just begged and sobbed and screamed at an image of her mother, but the sniffle is what she needed to feel self-conscious about. "I wasn't exactly a good person."

"You keep speaking of a strict binary. Time doesn't work the way you think it does. Neither does goodness. It's sort of a…" Aurora paused and loosened her hold. Susan let a small gap grow between them.

"Scale?" Susan offered. Aurora shook her head.

"No. It's more of a sphere. A sphere that takes a lot of things into account. Things like having a broken soul for a mother and growing up in a time where it was difficult to realize you even needed help."

"So, she *was* broken. My mother. Her soul. It was broken?"

"Yes. And I'm sorry."

"Do you…" Susan paused. She wasn't sure if she was allowed to ask this question. "Do you know what broke her?"

"It wasn't you." Aurora assured her. "And it wasn't the twin sisters your mother was forced to bury. No. She was broken before Susan Chambers was born." Susan nodded and took a deep breath even though she knew she didn't really need one. It just made her feel better to do it. The ice released its grip on her, her insides softening as they thawed.

Even as she felt herself center a bit, she was still just on the edge of trembling. Another unnecessary breath and she felt the chill pull a little further away. In the middle of her third grounding breath, something else occurred to Susan.

"What happened to my mother's soul? Can you tell me that?"

"Of course. Remember, once you decide what you want to do next and leave The Hall of Memories, everything you experienced as Susan Chambers will be forgotten. The slate wiped clean. I can answer any question you have ever had. And your mother's soul ceased to exist. It wasn't an old soul, but it had a good number of millennia drawing really short straws. The cracks had been forming for eons and, unfortunately, another life lived enduring abuse and neglect and it broke entirely during Elizabeth's lifetime."

"You knew she was breaking and you let her reincarnate anyway?"

"The soul was aware it was cracking. Yes. It gave it one more go. Cracks can heal. So can breaks. But not always. Hope is sometimes a false prophet."

"But what about the impact a broken or breaking soul has on others? Aren't there guard rails in place to keep one soul from tormenting another?"

"Well, no. There are no guard rails. What would those look like? How would we enforce them?" Aurora shrugged and shook her head in tiny little bobs. "I, we, those of us who guide souls through their After Deaths, have no power to affect their choices. We can force some moments of reckoning," she paused to offer a conciliatory glance, "but we can't ultimately do anything to interfere once a soul has made their choice. That would interfere with the free will each and every soul intrinsically possesses." Aurora might have sounded a little incredulous and Susan bristled.

"Every soul has complete and utter free will to do whatever it wants?" Susan was aghast. The anarchy and lawlessness that could erupt from that much unchecked freedom of choice was unsettling her.

"Yes. I mean, within the confines of the laws of biology and physics according to the world and universe you're beholden to, yes. Every soul in every iteration can make any choice it wants." Aurora lifted herself from the ground with a suave grace Susan might have envied when she was alive. Susan followed suit. "That's not to say there aren't consequences for those choices. You could have chosen to murder someone as Susan Chambers. And lots of outcomes would be made possible by that choice. But if you were successful and weren't caught, you'd have done exactly what you chose to do. Who, really, could have stopped you aside from perhaps the victim themself?"

"But now I've messed with someone else's free will by ending their life?"

"Have you? They had choices they could have made to."

"I'm pretty sure everyone wakes up in the morning and, by continuing to allow their heart to beat and their lungs to draw air, they are sort of subconsciously choosing to not get murdered."

Aurora bobbed her head. "Absolutely. I wouldn't argue that point. I mean there are exceptions to every absolute, but on the whole, yes. Most people choose not to get murdered, even if it isn't an active, verbally stated choice."

"That would mean my choice to murder is my fucking with their free will and choice to remain unmurdered."

"No." Aurora pronounced, her eyes inviting the inevitable challenge.

"No?" Susan let her eyes fall shut and held them there. Her hand lifted and she applied pressure to the bridge of her nose. This was like arguing with fresh marketing school graduates. Susan knew she was right but had to work extra hard to prove that. Because a degree trumps real world experience. Obviously.

"No," Aurora repeated. "Because the choices they made leading up to the moment you committed to murdering them could have prepared them to fend off the attack. Perhaps they chose to arm themselves and carry a concealed weapon." Aurora ticked off options on her fingers as she elaborated. "Perhaps they worked out and mastered a martial art. Perhaps they chose to stop for a coffee and missed the moment they first met you. Perhaps they never made whatever choice they made that led to you deciding to murder them. No choice happens in isolation."

"Okay, I'll concede there. But what choice could I have made as a literal infant to save myself from the wounding words of a broken soul?"

"Oh. Nothing. Your choice in that was not to allow or disallow what was done to you but what you did in response to it."

"I'm sorry?"

Aurora brought her hands together in a tent in front of her breastbone. She pressed her lips together, and this time searched the floor for answers instead of the ceiling.

"If you owned a house, and a hurricane came and blew that house away, whose choice was it to destroy your home?"

"No one's," Susan answered. "It was an act of nature or god or whatever forces rule the weather."

"Correct. As the homeowner, you might question the builder's choices, but you also had the opportunity, if perhaps not the resources, to have it inspected or reinforced. And even that might not have been enough. It was, as you said, an act of nature. The choice and the free will sometimes come in the aftermath."

"It wasn't my fault that my mother was the vessel for a broken soul, but it was my fault I didn't get enough therapy to not be a raging wad of dick cheese to almost everyone in my life?" Susan's head dipped and she knew she sounded incredulous.

Aurora laughed, the words slipping in between the giggles. "No. Not at all." Her laugh was high and keening. It sounded like birds twittering about the first flushes of spring, excited and enthusiastic. "Again. Whose fault is a hurricane? You keep trying to assign blame. The same way you can only hope a home can withstand a hurricane if you don't know anything about building or construction, some folks don't know what to do when confronted with a crisis, abuse, or neglect. You had free will, but that doesn't mean you had access to or even understanding of all your options.

"Your teachers, your peers, you coworkers, other victims of your abusers also had choices they could have made that may have helped you. Every soul has free will, but every soul is subject to influence from other souls' choices." Aurora looked expectant but must not have seen what she wanted to on Susan's face. Her eyes narrowed, then relaxed as she tried again. "If James' last victim had come forward, would he still have held the position to turn his attention on you? Perhaps not. But he also may not have been there to promote you either."

Susan pursed her lips as she considered Aurora's point. "It's the butterfly effect. Butterflies beating their wings in Brazil kick off a chain reaction of events that cause earthquakes to roll through Japan. Is that what you're saying?"

"In a sense. Yes." A tiny grin threatened Aurora's lips. "And no. The what-ifs of the lessons learned from a life lived are enough to drive anyone insane. What if your mom wasn't broken? You wouldn't have been the person who paid an assistant's student loans off, even if you did it for selfish reasons."

"There's no way to definitively say my life would have followed a different path with different parents. The abuse shaped my reactions but not my skills or talents." Susan countered.

Aurora's head wobbled on her neck while she considered Susan's point. "Alright. Fair enough. But let's say you'd reported James for his actions. You wouldn't have had the credentials to get your last job with the beautiful conference room where you paid the cleaning staff extra to clean the windows. And that series of events saved a child's life."

Susan felt her eyes go wide. "How so?"

Aurora crossed the room, approaching a frosted glass door. Leaning against the wall beside it, so she faced Susan once more, the guide explained. "All that cash you left, that money helped Luzia, the cleaner lady, pay her sister's and cancer-ridden niece's way to the States. Her niece was able to get treatments at St. Jude's. She survived the cancer because you wanted a spotless view of a pretty building. Not all the butterflies are making earthquakes. Some of them are making gentle rains that help flowers bloom and creeks carve tiny little paths through the forest floor. Destruction and creation are two sides of the same coin." Aurora looked at Susan expectantly. Though Susan wasn't sure what she was expected to do.

Not knowing what to say irked Susan so she said, "Can we have cake here? Like can we eat something as pure forms of energy?" Aurora said nothing, but the biggest grin pulled the apples of her cheeks up, her eyes crescent moons behind the mounds. "Yes. And no." Aurora gestured to the door she leaned next to.

"I thought we were done with the doors," Susan challenged.

"Indulge me."

Susan obliged and pushed the door open to find herself standing along one particular little curve of a Venetian canal. She sucked in air as realization settled.

They were at Sullaluna.

Sullaluna was half bistro, half bookshop in a beautiful corner of Venice. If Susan had a happy place, it was here. Aurora gestured to a table already set with steaming cups of rich, night-black espresso and plates of cakes. Susan loved French pastry, but the Italians had figured something out about making sweets no one had ever improved upon, in her experience.

Choosing the seat that looked toward the spired wall opposite the Sullaluna, Susan sat to find an espresso and a plate of a pear and chocolate farrow torte.

"*Torta di farro, pere e cioccolato.*" Susan crooned. Despite having visited Italy fourteen times since turning thirty, the only Italian Susan knew was about food and how to find food. She could order anything she wanted from any tucked-away eatery in the remotest places in Italy. But she couldn't ask where a library, bathroom, or bus stop was without the help of a pocket translator or a stroke of luck that someone nearby spoke English. With her nose that wasn't a nose, she inhaled deeply, losing herself entirely in the aromas of the sweetly tangy pears and the perfectly bitter chocolate. "I'm guessing I can't actually eat this."

Aurora seesawed her shoulders gently. "You won't be ingesting anything, no. But remember, I said you could be a cat if you could fully embrace everything it is to be a cat, right?" Susan nodded, fending off all-consuming thoughts about that cake. "The same goes for any experience. You can enjoy eating because you fully comprehend what it is to eat food, especially food you knew well and truly enjoyed. Like this cake. From this café. In Venice."

"Alright. You're forgiven," Susan said, grabbing the fork and letting it slip through the cake. The salivary glands she did not have kicked in as that bite approached her lips. Ladyhood be damned, she was going to be inappropriate about this. It was her After Death. Fuck 'em. And her mother, too.

"Oh. That's wonderful. What have you forgiven me for, though?" Aurora leaned forward slightly and rested her perfectly manicured nails, a taupe color that gently shifted to white at the tips, against the little *tazzina* before her.

"That was sort of intense back there. People pay therapists to avoid having that sort of violent confrontation with their trauma." Susan said before all her decorum poured out of her in the form of a moan. That cake hit her mouth and a purse of her lips had the pear brushing her tongue with the gentleness of a lover. Aurora had the decency to avert her gaze. When Susan was finished with that first perfect moment of blissful satisfaction and pried her eyes open once more, Aurora was staring at the statue of the

Virgin Mary holding the Christ Child standing vigil on the wall to her left.

Without looking back to Susan and her cake, she said, "We're not trying to give you therapy. You no longer have to heal. You just have to understand in what ways you were left broken. Sometimes, the lessons of that life lived are hidden in those fissures." Aurora looked back at Susan as her words floated out over the canal.

"But if you don't heal the damage a soul endured between one life and the next, isn't that how cracks are formed? And don't those cracks spider and spread until you end up with souls like the one that didn't escape Elizabeth Elaine's existence without breaking?"

"Admittedly, I can't say that doesn't happen. But I can reasonably assume that's not the case most of the time." Susan almost kissed the next bite before letting it fill her. Aurora continued, undisturbed. "How does one polish a gem? You add grit and pressure over time. It polishes and shines and enhances the beauty that has taken all of history to create. Lives that struggled with and through trauma are no less important to a soul's understanding of existence."

The velvet texture of the cake didn't melt in Susan's mouth; it dissolved like effervescent air, painting its essence across the soft, slick tissue of her inner cheek. A growl of satiation rose up from Susan's throat as Aurora elaborated further.

"The only time a soul can examine the traumas it experienced is after they can no longer be hurt by the source of that trauma. Sometimes, the only way to understand what caused all the pain is to examine it after the pain is gone, or at least not increasing. Some souls have resources and support to do it during the once-traumatic existence. Some souls, like yours, remain unable process any of it until they experience the After Death."

Susan savored the last caresses of the *dolci* on her palette and considered Aurora. "And you're claiming that a soul that experiences trauma isn't always ruined?" Susan glided her fork across the smooth mounded edge of the plate, sweeping the final crumbs of satisfaction into a pile. Pressing the back of her fork into the last remnants, she slid the steel into her mouth, twirling her tongue around the tines for every last molecule of pleasure the cake could offer. She was greedy for it and didn't care. Aurora pressed on.

"That's exactly what I'm claiming. Souls that lived hard, painful, traumatic lives are not necessarily broken by those experiences. Many are fortified and more resilient in the face of future hardships. Souls must endure those rough, unfair, difficult existences to understand all that life is and is not."

Susan, her cake consumed, leaned back until her shoulder blades found the scrawling wrought-iron vines that tangled themselves into the chair back. "You can't have the good without the bad? Is that what you're saying?" She crossed her arms across her chest, throwing her legs out and crossing her ankles. She tipped her face to the Italian sun and felt its warmth kiss her cheeks in greeting. *Ciao amore mio*, it whispered against her skin. Aurora laughed again. Susan let herself drink in the sound.

"If you need to distill it down that far, it's not wrong. It's simple, but not wrong. At its core, this is one of those 'the universe seeks balance' ideas. You can't have dark without light or good without bad. All things must have an equal and opposite." A clinking sound opened Susan's eyes. Aurora used her fork to push bits of her cake around as she explained further. "In order to understand and appreciate those altruistic lessons, you have to know to what they are superior. What is the opposite of giving?"

Susan considered before offering, "Selfishness?"

Aurora nodded. "Would you continue to give if no one was ever selfish?" The guide paused, her eyebrows reaching for her hairline. "You might want to, but if absolutely no one is selfish, the problem no longer exists. No one needs anything given to them. The wealth or opportunity or aid is simply available because no one is hoarding an unnecessary portion out of avarice or self-fulfillment. And if you can't give, how do you continue to perpetuate the idea of giving as the whole concept fades into obscurity?"

"That's incredibly utopian. Almost to the point of falla-cious." Susan said, righting herself in the chair once more. Her eyes fell upon the wide mouth of her tazzino.

"Perhaps. But why does any soul ever, no matter their spe-cies, genotype, or state of matter, strive to be good or nice or kind or respectful? Why does any soul have to give a single fuck about any other soul?" Susan paused mid-sip at Aurora's impressive use of the word 'fuck.' She finished her sip as she considered her answer.

"If souls are people, and people are their souls, then the life I just lived has to enjoy similar basic motivations to everyone else's, right? Not fame and fortune, per se, but baser, instinctual motivations. A way to protect your physi-cal form. A way to protect the soul that physical form houses." Susan drug a long sip of espresso through her teeth. She felt the fluid burble and skip across her tongue, the bittersweet aromas flooding her sinuses. Technically improper, but again: Her After Death. She would do it however she wanted, and she liked pulling it through her teeth once it had cooled down a little more. It made it feel satiny in her mouth.

Aurora sipped at her espresso idly. "Yes. That's accurate enough. No matter what sort of existence a soul experi-ences, those two motivations are fairly ubiquitous."

"Then I'd say one way a soul could protect itself is by con-necting and interacting with souls. As humans, we don't want to be lonely. We strive not to be and really, truly struggle when we are. Some souls need more points of connection than others, I'd guess. At least from the human perspective, people have different social preferences. Loners, introverts, class clowns, extroverts. Lots of labels exist to describe how people interact with one another."

"Alright. So is connection or relationship reason enough to strive to be 'good' as opposed to 'bad'?"

Susan didn't have to think about this answer. "Yeah. I think it is. I'm not so egotistical to think I figured this out ten seconds ago, but the need for connection is probably the most important reason people choose to be good, even if it's easier to be mean or hateful or ignorant." Susan swirled the cup, watching the deep brown liquid stain the porcelain before sliding back down to the bottom. "And since the most fulfilling road is also the harder road, you must convince yourself over and over again that it's worth choosing goodness. I think that's where we get the idea of legacy. If you're good you'll leave a legacy that will, hopefully, inspire others to be good. Which will help keep those you were connected to safe. They made you feel safe and seen." Aurora cocked her head to the side, listening intently to Susan's revelation. "In exchange, you make them safe and seen. Relationships, the best ones, are a little symbiotic, I guess. You gather other souls just as they gather you, forever pushing forward to preserve the legacy, the protection of souls intertwined and cooperating."

"And what about the 'every hero needs a villain' trope? The balance?" Aurora tapped a taupe nail against the cup, a subtle, heady ping skipping off the Venetian stones. Susan nodded, surprised she had a response ready.

"Every villain is the hero of their own story. They're still pursuing the same protections of their physical form and the soul inside it. What is right and wrong might misalign, but both sides think they're striving to be good." Susan pulled the last sip of her espresso into her mouth and swished it gently across each cheek. Left. Then right. And then it was gone. Susan was not sad it was gone. She was pleased she'd been able to cherish it one last time. She was satisfied.

Aurora offered one final challenge. "Does that mean there's no such thing as evil?"

Susan smirked. "Think of it more like a sphere."

Aurora shrugged and her eyes drifted upward. Susan knew she wasn't admiring the cloudless sapphire field of the Italian sky. When her eyes focused on Susan once more, Aurora offered, "To be fair, what feels like your sudden deeper understanding of the idea and motivation of a soul is a normal part of The After Death. The further you get from the moment of your physical form expiring, the more the knowledge your soul has garnered from previous iterations sort of…" Aurora made that swirling motion with her hand, "…catches up to you."

"You said we don't remember our past lives. Not truly."

"You don't. Not the memories. But the lessons stay with you. Those become clearer. I can't confirm, but I've heard that in the moment a soul completely ends one iteration and begins another one, there is a singular moment in which a soul experiences true clarity. It remembers everything it has learned from its past lives and adds its shiny new lesson to the collection." Aurora inhaled deeply, her face serene, her shoulders squared. "What lesson did you learn as Susan Chambers?"

It was Susan's turn to gaze upward. But she *was* looking at the sky. She gazed into the endless blue and, for the first time, noticed it wasn't just a monotone of deep cyan. With nothing more important to do than observe the sky that had overseen her most peaceful moments of existence, she noticed the faint ribbons of variation. Swathes of azure and cerulean swept across acres of cobalt with blossoming patches of sapphire throughout.

"Is it too lazy to say 'balance'?" Susan tried.

"Balance is a perilous lesson to learn. I don't think it's a lazy ideal." Susan's guide confirmed. "Can you expand the concept though?"

"I tried to reconcile a lot of accounts, not all of them my responsibility, but I tried, nonetheless. I may not have always been cognizant of the impact of my choices, but more than once did a choice that served me also benefit another. There was balance. I might have been obtuse about it, but I was putting good into the world. As much as I might want and arguably need to apologize for those choices that hurt more than served, there's balance in those as well."

Aurora only nodded at this, still and attentive. Susan resumed her explanation.

"That's not a justification for being shitty, to be clear. I wasn't a good person." Susan's hand flew up to stop Aurora's protest. "Not all the way. But neither was I an all-the-way bad person. I was morally neutral." Susan paused and chewed on her lip that she didn't have. "I think the idea of balance means that you have to have a fulcrum there in the center. Maybe Susan Chambers' experience was as the fulcrum. One side was kinda shitty, but the other side wasn't so bad. Neither side was the worst or best version of herself, her soul, or humanity. And that's fine." Susan shrugged. "It feels a little anti-climactic, I guess. But it's…" Susan lifted her hands, palms to the multi-tonal sky and shrugged like a cartoon character, "…neutral." The last word tumbled out of her in the form of a chuckle.

"Are you ready to move on from being the morally neutral Susan Chambers and experience something or someone or someway new?" Aurora asked expectantly. "Would you like to peruse a catalogue of options we think best suit your soul's journey so far, because we—" Susan cut her off.

"Without knowing my options, is it unreasonable to want to go back to being a human? Is there some sort of bias incurred with humanity that makes that a weird choice? An internalized -ism or something?"

Aurora chuckled and smiled broadly. "No. That's not weird. A lot of souls spend quite a few cycles in the same sort of realm of species and universe." Aurora turned her head and her eyes drifted up again. "Yes, we can send you back to Earth as a human again. I guess you could say you're in your Human Era."

"Did you just make a Taylor Swift joke?" Susan asked, letting her head tip to the side and her eyebrows knit together.

"I did. And I won't apologize for it. Her art is ageless. And I would know. Ready?"

"Wait." Susan said, serious one last time. "Can you pull any strings or see if you can get at least one normal parent for this next one? Yes, I understand that trauma has lessons to offer, but like…" Susan trailed off, looking for a way to request this for herself without sounding selfish. She couldn't find one, so she leaned into it instead. "Maybe we can try not to start all the traumatizing as a child? I know that's selfish, but I'm still technically Susan Chambers. She was selfish. And sometimes her selfishness helped others. I'm just trying to help this next kid out a little."

Aurora smiled gently, her eyes doing that crinkle-corner thing again. "I'll see what I can do. It was an honor to guide you through your After Death, Susan Chambers."

"Thank you for your patience. Oh, and thanks for the coffee, Aurora." Susan lifted herself from the chair and took a deep breath. Looking down at her guide, she added, "I didn't mention it, but your outfit is perfect. *Sei assolutamente stupenda.*"

The world shimmered in a million colors Susan had never known existed, and just before it winked out entirely, Susan heard Aurora say from far, far away, "*Sì, ti piacerà davvero questa prossima vita, signora Camerino.*"

ACKNOWLEDGMENTS

The acknowledgements are my very favorite part of a book. It's like for just one second you get to see the inner workings of an author's life. The people who are important to them and the impact those people had on the author who created the story I just finished reading. It's kind of cool what just a list of mushy stuff does for me.

Anywho, here we go.

First to Jack. I need you to know that while I'll type this in the back of a book, I'll never have the courage to say it out loud. You're the reason I didn't quit. You're the reason I kept trying to work around the screaming voice of my past telling me I couldn't do this. I couldn't write good stories and I couldn't get anyone to care. We've stood in the garage, and you patiently let me call myself names and then lovingly corrected each one. I'm still following my dreams because you're too stubborn to let me quit. You see what's inside and you love it, and I am astounded. Thank you.

Jennifer and Emily. You read everything I write and are my biggest cheerleaders. My imposter syndrome hates you, but I love you. Keeping doing it. I wish I didn't need these two external voices of acceptance and approval, but I do. And I'm lucky you two are mine.

Amy. At no point did you have to give all the help you gave. But I'm so glad you did. Self-publishing is heavy work, and you lightened the load. Thank you.

To my editors, alpha & beta readers, and everyone who I just randomly stopped and forced you to listen to a thing I just wrote and helped me work out kinks in the process. Thank you. Thank you. A million times thank you.

To my kids, I'm sorry I'm not providing you a boatload of trauma like Susan's mom. However will you develop a wicked sense of humor if your mom is trying really hard not to suck? Sorry.